The Abaddon Letters & Other Stories.

Colin Midhe

For anyone who knows
What's in the basement.

The Abaddon Letters

"I do not accuse the Heavens or any other, nor do I intend to lament so ill a lot,

because to evil more than to good I am wonted,

but if I must pass through the gates of Hell to that good you have spoken of, I am

willing."

Niccolò Machiavelli

April

"Drake"

I am here.
They have brought me here, and I don't think I can leave
At least, that's what they tell me

His name is Jeremy Weber
He will be my therapist
while I am here
I don't trust him and don't
know why I should

Pills
They want me to take pills

But pills will change me

I am Luo. Joka-jok.

My grandmother's name was Awiti Ochieng. Her mother during the birth, and left Grandmother on the stone steps of a church. The missionaries took her with them to America, and she married a man named Andrew Kenway. My mother, born of them, was half-Luo. She married another African man, whose family had been here since slavery, and they had me. I am one-quarter Luo. That is what the certificate of my birth will tell you.

But Luo is not something that exists in halves, or in quarters. Luo is all of you.

I don't want to write anymore, but Jeremy
Weber tells me I must. He says I should
introduce myself.

I was born Marianna DeWitt. I am twenty-one
years old.

I am here because I fell in love with a
woman.

<u>12 April.</u>

I am told to keep this journal because writing has had therapeutic effects on other patients. I've never been much of a writer, but I will do what I can. I do want to get better. I don't want to suffer anymore. ~~Living without her is~~

Dr. Weber asked me to describe the pain. I don't know what to say.

<u>13 April.</u>

I know how to describe it.

It's an albatross. It is hung around my neck, a constant reminder. The albatross is the single great symbol of karmic law; when we take action, we must irrevocably live with the repercussions

I loved her. I loved her knowing that all of society would turn hard eyes on me and name me pervert, heathen. Our love was beautiful. But I wore it as an albatross around my neck. I was given the greatest love in the world, and the world's hatred was my penance.

I don't want to write anymore.

They can't make me.

Fine.

<u>25 April.</u>

$N = R f_s f_p n_e f_1 f_i f_c L$
where R is rate of avg. star formation, f_s is fraction of
stars that have planetary systems, f_p is no. stars that have
planets, n_e is planets within the ecoshell, f_1 is no. planets
that could actually support life, f_i is no. planets that
could support civilizations (ergo intelligent life), f_c is
the fraction of those civilizations that are able to transmit
the news of their existence into space, and L is the length
of time for which they release those signals

N gives the number of civilizations we should be listening
to.

<u>26 April.</u>

We, humans, are searching for extra-terrestrial intelligence.
In 1961, at the Green Bank facility, Dr. Drake presented his
marvelous equation. She used to recite it with stars in her
eyes. But then her face would fall, just a little, and she'd
say

But then we must account for the Fermi paradox. If they're
out there, Marianna, why can't we hear them?

I don't know. But I know she's out there, even if I can't
hear her now. I cannot see her, or touch her, or hear her
voice, but I know she exists.

~~At least I think I do~~

<u>27 April.</u>

I look African. This is what Jeremy Weber tells me.

My mother told me I look Luo.

The other inmates tell me I look like a nigger.

My reflection tells me I look like me.

I do not know who is most correct.

28 April.

I may not be here just because of her. When she left, I put a

bullet in my brain. (I lived.) That is probably why they insist I

stay. And I suppose I do not blame them.

29 April.

The routine course of treatment for homosexuality is electroshock therapy. Jeremy Weber would like to try corrective therapy first. I will be shown pictures of the female genitalia, and pictures and video of females engaging in sexual activity, while being forced to vomit.

This is corrective. Healthy.

So they say.

30 April.

My therapy begins today.

My entry from the twenty-fifth of April regards the Drake Equation. Her eyes themselves looked like stars when she recited it for me. I don't understand the equation, and never have, but I have memorized it, because she used to murmur it in her sleep.

N gives the number of civilizations we should be hearing.

May

"Shiloh"

I cannot focus

                          My writing is

                        Badly distorted

                            Broken

                          I cannot

                  It is the first day of spring?

2 May.

Colors are too vibrant. Too bright.

They did electroshock first. Why?

E

Elec

Electro

Electroshock

Electro

Elec

E

Every

Everywhere

Every

E

End

3 May.

My mind returns to me in bits and pieces. I still see her. I won't tell Jeremy Weber. I want to remain intact.

4 May.

Regarding the bullet from my entry on the twenty-eighth of April. I still have it. I used to wear it in a little bag around my neck (it was taken from me, of course, when I was admitted). When Jeremy Weber asked why, I informed him thus:

This bullet is my past. My past tried to kill me. It cannot do so anymore, and is no threat, but still I wear it, as an albatross.

Jeremy Weber didn't understand. Much to his chagrin,

    the African-Luo-Nigger-Me is much better read than he.

5 May.

The Luo came to Kenya in pieces. The Joka-jok came first, then the Jo-k'Owiny, then the Jok'Omolo, then the Abasuba. It was a point of pride for Awiti Ochieng, my grandmother, that the Joka-jok came first. The place they arrived in is now called Lake Victoria.

I have never been there. Not my Luo part, and not my American part. None of me but my heart.

6 May.

    Sheol is naked before him, and Abaddon has no covering.

                             Job 26:6

Those who do not wear the seal of God on their foreheads will be tormented by Abaddon for five months. Five months. Five months.

Tell me not that Jeremy Weber is my Abaddon.

<u>7 May.</u>

When my grandmother, Awiti Ochieng, came to America from Kenya, she was a very small child, only three. She told me that she could feel the darkness even then. It consumed her, she said.

The darkness is clinical. Some of the inmates here complain of it. I know it, too, though only because I lost Shiloh. Before that, for me, at least, it was a non-entity.

> I know more of that abyss than I should like, more than is safe.

> I believe that abyss, that darkness, to be Abaddon.

<u>8 May.</u>

Regarding my entry from the sixth of May, which Dr. Weber should like very much to know more about.

(A note: I didn't realize Dr. Weber was reading this journal. One of the orderlies removes it from my room and brings it to him while I sleep. I don't know why this didn't occur to me. If you are reading this, Dr. Weber, this invasion of my privacy is uncalled for. If you wanted to know my thoughts, you had but to ask.)

Abaddon is Biblical. (My mother loved the Bible, and Christ, and worshiped on every Sunday and Wednesday, and marked my forehead on Ash Wednesday so that the DEVIL would never find me.) Abaddon is either an angel or a place of infernal darkness; he is, perhaps, both.

In the Mesoretic texts of the Hebrew bible, Abaddon is the opposite of Sheol. Some believe it is the damned land of fire and snow, visited once by Moses in Gehenna.

In the homily by Timothy, Abaddon was tasked by G-d to collect the earth with which G-d would make Adam. Abaddon, then, was our Creator before G-d. Of all the earth in all of Creation, Abaddon chose the earth that made Adam.

Or Abaddon is hell. The Jews and the Christians agree on little, and on this point they argue still, through text if not through words.

9 May.

Her name is Shiloh. Shiloh St. Claire. I fell in love with her name first. Her name is poetry.

An addendum to my previous entry: in the Acts of Thomas, Abaddon and the DEVIL are one and the same.

10 May.

Corrective therapy began today. Rather, Dr. Weber attempted to begin it. He began by showing me a picture of Shiloh. I was so overcome I could not continue, and was removed from the room and sedated. It is now evening, and still there is cotton behind my skull, white noise in my mind.

I hope Shiloh is well, that she is happy teaching in New Orleans. If there was ever a place for a woman and her Luo beloved, it is there. I hope she gets to meet Dr. Drake, that they may discuss that marvelous equation.

11 May.

I am still recovering from the sedative. I was given too high a dose.

I shall take the time to remark about some of the other inmates. I have found an unlikely friend in one Mrs. Edwina Bernstein, a woman of middling age who has lost much of her hair. Her eyes are mismatched, one blue and one green. She tells me he is here because she hears voices, but her eyes sparkle with mischief when she says so. I think she may be lying- in this case, a lie by omission, because I still do not know why she is here. She asked me the the purpose for my stay (as if this were an inn!) and I answered thus:

I am but a poor visitor from Sodom.

She laughed long and hard at that, and told me that she loved a girl once. She would tell me no more; an orderly overheard our conversation, and reminded us that our ailments are only to be discussed with Dr. Weber.

Shame. I should have liked to hear about Edwina's Shiloh.

12 May.

I should remark that Dr. Weber's use of electroshock therapy for homosexual patients is outdated by a decade at least. Public opinion on homosexuality is changing quickly. Perhaps Dr. Weber should make an attempt to un-mire himself from

15 May.

They did it again. The electroshock. Still hard to think. Hand shakes badly

16 May.

Shiloh

That is all for now. I just wanted to see her name.

<u>17 May.</u>

ShilohShilohShiloh

Holihs

Lihohs

Holish

Hilosh

Silohh

<u>18 May.</u>

Regarding my entry from the twelfth of May. I was interrupted because I was abruptly escorted to therapy. I am, of course, beholden to Dr. Weber's courses of treatment, but in the future should like to be given the opportunity to finish my writing first.

Dr. Weber should un-mire himself from the past. Unless he would like an albatross of his own.

<u>19 May.</u>

About my grandmother, Awiti Ochieng.

She came to America, as I have said, at the age of three, with a pair of missionaries, a husband and wife- Mr. and Mrs. Paul Connelly. (I cannot remember the wife's first name; she was only ever Mrs. Paul Connelly to me.) The first thing they did, upon arriving in America, was give my grandmother a Christian first name. Therefore, her full name is Hannah Awiti Ochieng Connelly. When she became pregnant with my mother at fifteen, the Connellys cast my grandmother from their home, and she became Awiti Ochieng again. Luo again. When she was sixteen, and six months pregnant, she married the baby's father, Andrew Kenway, who was then twenty-seven, and became Awiti Kenway (it is traditional among the Luo, as among Americans, for a woman to take her husband's name). To the child they gave a Luo name- Aburu, meaning 'born during a funeral.' When Andrew Kenway asked my grandmother why they should name their child should be named so, she responded thus:

Today marks the death of the woman I would have been.

<u>20 May.</u>

Dr. Weber has asked that I continue to write about my family. Because he has asked, I am uncomfortable doing so. I shall write about something else.

I learned the other day that plants grow in the direction of sunlight. Edwina is a botanist, and a biologist. She sketched me a tree she saw once, growing among much taller specimens in a rain forest in the Congo, that had grown in a spiral. She told me thus:

> The trees growing around it, you see, grew densely packed, obscuring most of the sunlight, save for small patches that would break through the canopy. So this little fellow here, this twisted tree, would grow toward the shifting patches of sunlight as the year progressed.

Despite the twist in its trunk, the tree eventually grew tall enough that it could reach the sunlight, wherever it fell, and began to grow straight up-and-down, like its larger, stronger companions.

Edwina allowed me to keep the sketch of the tree- perhaps because she saw the tears in my eyes. It was the most beautiful thing I had ever seen.

21 May.

Today is Shiloh's birthday. She is thirty years old. The difference of nine years between us did not make it any easier for us to be public about our relationship. We met when I was eighteen, during my first year at university. She was the assistant teacher for one of my literature classes. Shiloh has a scientific mind, but she and the professor got along particularly well, and she somewhat reluctantly agreed to teach with him.

I am so glad she did.

And so sad.

22 May.

I thought a lot yesterday about the thirty years Shiloh has spent on this planet, and about my fleeting presence in them. I know our three years meant as much to her as they did to me. I know she didn't leave because she didn't love me. She just had to be free. Free of this place, and its poisons.

She drug her roots up from the ground and ran to find her
    sunlight, and I was too afraid to follow.

<u>23 May.</u>

We heard awful screaming from a male inmate as he was taken
to the ward today. Something about the DEVIL.

                        Abaddon again

<u>24 May.</u>

There are few women scientists of particular note in this day and age. Shiloh and I spent our time together waiting for the world to catch up. She would remark, with a smile brighter than sunshine, that I am still young, and youth means anger.

You're angry, too, I'd say. Angry they don't take you
       seriously.

She would laugh.

        Yes. It's the brain that makes the scientist, not the
        vagina, not the breasts. Those are just an added bonus.

I hope that today's little girls will grow into tomorrow's women scientists. I hope that women like Shiloh carve that path open for them. I hope they find sunlight all their own.

I will be here,

 in the dark.

<u>25 May.</u>

I have finally agreed to take the pills. If only because the pain of missing Shiloh is more than I can bear.

<u>26 May.</u>

The side effects of the medication will take time to manifest. I am so afraid.

<u>27 May.</u>

More therapy today— not electroshock, thank Abaddon, if He is listening. Dr. Weber again showed me the picture of Shiloh. I began to cry, but there was no need for sedation. I was in control. I am still in control. He says my desire to be released must surpass my desire to be with her once more.

Perhaps he is right.

The darkness of which Awiti Ochieng spoke. I think I know it now. I think I knew it then, too.

I have said it is clinical. It affects many inmates here, many. It affects, particularly, a girl named Sophie, who sits by the window in the common room day in and day out, with her hair lank around her shoulders and her arms around her knees. I find her beautiful, but I look on her like a mother looks on a child, because I see so much of myself in her brokenness.

Brokenness is beautiful, too. We are all, here, broken
    people.

Because I have written about Edwina and Sophie, Dr. Weber has asked that I write, too, about some of the other inmates.

There is a girl here named Lian. She is Chinese in descent; I believe her parents are immigrants. They have visited her once, and looked confused when the orderlies addressed them in English. Lian translated. She is here because she shot the man who raped her. She shot him twelve times in the head. (Well, three times in the head, nine times into the bloody, pulpy remains of a rapist's brain.) She evicted him from the world of the living, liberated the world from his presence. I do not blame her. For all that has happened to her, she maintains a smile most days. She loves poetry, so we have much to talk about.

Another girl— no, a woman— is Carmen. She is Latina. Her family has lived in California for six generations. She declares proudly that she is an American. Her grandfather built his own architecture firm from the ground up, worked three jobs to put himself through school and become licensed. Carmen says she is the product of the American dream, and I am inclined to agree. She was studying to become a lawyer when she was ~~imprisoned~~ admitted. Her ailment is unclear to me. There is a wildness in her, certainly— a power that must be terrifying to the men who would see her fail. All of the girls here are powerful.

(It smacks of conspiracy.)

If we are here, we cannot be out there, in their world, taking what they have long enjoyed.

There are a disproportionate number of women of color here. Chinese, Latina, Vietnamese, Chilean.

Luo.

I find a strange comfort in it. In here, in this prison for those with demons in their minds, I am not a stranger in a white world.

But still no place for both me and Shiloh.

30 May.

To my grandmother, their daughter was Aburu Kenway Ochieng. To my grandfather, their daughter was Aburu Ochieng Kenway. And I believe this about sums up their dispute over how to raise their first child.

My mother had two little brothers. They were both given Christian names, white names— Jacob and Jordan. Mama told me that she and my grandmother, with their Luo names, sometimes felt like strangers in their own home. Outsiders.

Jordan was darker even than my mother; Jacob could almost pass as white. I have never met my Uncle Jacob. He cut himself free of our family before I was even born. His legal name is Jacob T. Kenway. The T, I am told, stands for nothing. It is only a T.

~~I think it stands for traitor.~~

But my Uncle Jordan was my kindest and most loyal friend when I was a little girl. He brought me candy and let me eat it before supper, but only if Mama's back was turned. He went to Kenya on several occasions, to Lake Victoria, and brought me back jewelry hand-crafted by the women who lived there, who still lived by the old ways, for whom the world of the Luo is alive and breathing and vibrant and dynamic, not a fragment of stories told at the dinner table.

Luo is all of me, but it is a me I do not know.

31 May.

Yesterday I saw Shiloh at the visitor's desk, arguing with an orderly.

I do not know if she was real, but it was so good to see her.

June

"Arecibo"

<u>1 June.</u>

Edwina showed me something fascinating today. Last year, Dr. Frank Drank and Mr. Carl Sagan sent a message into space using the new Arecibo telescope in Puerto Rico. The design graphically depicts our numbers 1-10, the atomic numbers of several cardinal elements, the nucleotides in DNA, etc. It is designed to tell others who is living on Earth, what we know.

Here is the Arecibo Message:

```
00000010101010000000000
00101000001010000000100
10001000100010010110010
10101010101010100100100
00000000000000000000000
00000000000011000000000
00000000001101000000000
00000000001101000000000
00000000010101000000000
00000000011111000000000
00000000000000000000000
11000011100011000011000
10000000000000110010000
11010001100011000011010
11111011111011111011111
00000000000000000000000
00010000000000000000010
00000000000000000000000
00001000000000000000001
11111000000000000011111
00000000000000000000000
11000011000011100011000
10000000100000000010000
11010000110001110011010
11111011111011111011111
00000000000000000000000
00010000001100000000010
00000000001100000000000
00001000001100000000001
11111000001100000011111
00000000001100000000000
00100000000100000000100
00010000001100000001000
00001100001100000010000
00000011000100001100000
00000000001100110000000
```

```
0000000110001000011000000
0000110000110000001000 0
0001000000100000001000
00100000001100000000100
01000000001100000000100
01000000000100000001000
00100000001000000010000
00010000000000001100000
00001100000000110000000
00100011101011000000000
00100000001000000000000
00100000111110000000000
00100001011101001011011
00000010011100100111111
10111000011100000110111
00000000010100000111011
00100000010100000111111
00100000010100000110000
00100000110110000000000
00000000000000000000000
00111000001000000000000
00111010100010101010101
00111000000000101010100
00000000000000101000000
00000000111110000000000
00000011111111100000000
00001110000000111000000
00011000000000001100000
00110100000000010110000
01100110000000110011000
01000101000001010001000
01000100100010010001000
00000100010100010000000
00000100001000010000000
00000100000000010000000
00000001001010000000000
01111001111101001111000
```

And if that isn't clear as day, I don't know what is.

3 June.

It was actually Shiloh. It was really Shiloh.

Dr. Weber told me she has been here seven times now. She has been trying to find me for six months, ever since I shot myself. My mother wrote her to tell her what happened.

Shiloh is trying to find me. She wants to see me. I am so happy I may die.

As punishment, Dr. Weber has prescribed another round of electroshock therapy.

4 June.

I am not

I am

I am not

I am

Iamnot

IamnotIamnotIamnotIamnotaniggerIamnotIamLUOIam

IamnotIamnotIamnotIamnotiamnotiamnotiamnotiamnot

IamnotIamnotIamnotIamnotiamnotiamnotiamnotiamnot

IamnotIamnotIamnotIamnotiamnotiamnotiamnotiamnot

IamnotIamnotIamnotIamnotiamnotiamnotiamnotiamnot

IamnotIamnotIamnotIamnotiamnotiamnotiamnotiamnot

IamnotIamnotIamnotIamnotiamnotiamnotiamnotiamnot

IamnotIamnotIamnotIamnotiamnotiamnotiamnotiamnot

IamnotIamnotIamnotIamnotiamnotiamnotiamnotiamnot

IamnotIamnotIamnotIamnotiamnotiamnotiamnotiamnot.

                                              I am.

Aren't I?

<u>5 June.</u>

Abaddon, I saw Abaddon, I was burdened by the albatross around my neck, and I could not stop him when he lifted Shiloh in his arms, carried her away.

When Virgil asked Dante if he wanted to see Hell, Dante went without hesitation, into the Inferno.

Did Shiloh receive the Arecibo message? Does she know where I am, what I am made of, that I

<u>6 June.</u>

There are burns in my skin. A symptom of the electroshock therapy. A side effect. A necessary evil. They are red and raw and painful. Lian helped me apply aloe. It is like water, sweeter and clearer than any mountain stream, soothing.

Lian told me about China. She has been twice— once when she was just a little girl, once the year after she completed senior high school. The second time she went alone, and walked all over the country that shaped her parents and, by extension, her. She saw its wonders and its tragedies. She let it become a part of her again.

I am so envious. I want to see Lake Victoria. I am Luo, Joka-jok. Lake Victoria is my place. It is what my bones are made of. Its waters are my blood. Its stories are my past. I wish my grandmother had never left. I wish I were not as I am.

Edwina Bernstein also belonged somewhere once. There is also a country that is a part of her. It is Germany. But it is a part of her in a different way than Kenya is part of me, and China a part of Lian, and her mismatched eyes darken to speak of it. She says that Germany is the reason for her eyes, actually. She says that her green eye is green with the naivete of youth, the color of a new sapling, but her blue eye has seen the reality of this world and has become aged and wise and cold, and has taken the color of an ancient ocean.

I believe her.

7 June.

What does it mean to BELONG?

I BELONGed with Shiloh.

I BELONGed with my grandmother and Mama.

I BELONG with the Luo.

I BELONG in Kenya.

I BELONG in New Orleans.

I BELONG in this place.

I am in pieces, and all of me BELONGs to something else. I want to BELONG to myself.

8 June.

Dr. Weber looked up the albatross. He told me it was a most elegant metaphor. I laughed long and hard at that. Only those who carry an albatross understand. There is no elegance in it. That great bird bends and twists our backs into grotesque malformations of the human figure. It splits us at the spine, and our brains dribble from our broken vertebrae.

Elegance indeed. What that man carries around his neck is little more than a hummingbird.

9 June.

That clinical darkness. I keep trying to write on it, and always my thoughts wander.

My grandmother said that the darkness is not a non-entity. It is a person. It is a person who sits in the very back of your mind. You know nothing of this person. This person has no name and no face. But this person dearly and desperately wants to see you dead. This person wants to see you prone on the floor. This person wants to see your life bleed away. The person is always there, when you are waking, when you sleep. When you close your eyes, the person creeps closer. If you sleep, the person may take possession of your mind and use it to kill your body.

Dr. Weber uses the term 'depression.' Depression. Darkness. Abaddon. They are all one and the same. The good doctor says that depression is an obstacle that can be overcome by faith. He says that it can build a person up from nothing, make them strong.

He's wrong. Abaddon gives no strength and cares nothing for faith. He only knows how to break. He cannot inspire the faithful, only create broken people. Husks. Eviscerated shells.

When my beloved Uncle Jordan shot himself in the head, I believe it was because his person had won. Abaddon has him now. Both of them.

10 June.

Carmen, apparently, suffers from nymphomania. We sat down and talked about our ailments. She says sex feels as natural for her as breathing. She says it makes her feel alive. Dr. Weber has asked her a thousand times if she was abused as a child. She always tells him no, and I believe that this is the truth. Ultimately, Carmen owns her body. It is hers. It connects her to her world, to other people. I think there is something beautiful and visceral in that. In any case, she didn't self-admit. Her parents forced her to come here. They are old Catholics, and believe her to be possessed by the DEVIL.

They're right, Carmen said, laughing. But the DEVIL didn't make her love sex. Sex did.

While Carmen and I spoke, sweet little Sophie got up from her spot on the windowsill and ran to her room. A coldness settled in my stomach, something arctic. Like ice. I think I know why she is here.

11 June.

I met my Uncle Jacob T. Kenway today.

He came to the asylum with a briefcase and several documents. Awiti Ochieng's will was found in a storage unit among her personal belongings. The new owners were cleaning out the unit and thought the single box should go to my grandmother's next of kin. Because Mama is, of course, nowhere to be found, the next of kin is Uncle Jacob.

At least, that is how I understand the situation. I was too busy watching his mouth move, watching those pinkish lips making words colored by condemnation. He looks down his nose at me. That nose is too broad for a white person, but he almost passes for a white man. I don't know if that makes him lucky or pitiful. (Both)

Uncle Jacob says that Grandmother left everything to me. 'Everything' once meant a fair bit of money, but Mama spent it a long time ago. I have been given Awiti Ochieng's cardboard box, the vesicle for all that remains of her life.

Except, I suppose, for my blood and my bones and my DNA.

I signed the documents to verify that I had received the box. It was taken away by an orderly. Uncle Jacob left. He did not hug me or touch me or tell me it was nice to meet me. But, to be fair, neither did I.

Dr. Weber would like to know where Mama is. I told him I don't know. He asked me to think very hard. I did, but I still don't know. He asked me why I was sent to the detention center when I was a little girl. I repeat that I don't know, and moreover, I've never been to a detention center, unless this hellish place counts.

He frowned, wrote in his notebook, and said we were done for the day.

13 June.

Sophie spoke to me. Not with words, but with her eyes. She sat down beside me on the couch in the recreation room and asked me— her eyes did, her sweet questioning gaze— what I was writing. I told her it is my journal, and asked if she'd like to add to it— a poem, perhaps. Her gaunt cheeks turned very pink, and she hurried away. It was the most lively I have seen her since coming here. Edwina agrees.

Edwina told me more about herself— more importantly, about Germany. She is a Jew. I guessed that much, but to see her say it, with the darkness in her eyes, made my heart ache. I took her in my arms and held her a long time, and though she didn't cry, I felt her thin shoulders tremble. It's been thirty years, she says, but she can still hear the screaming. She can still smell burning flesh, hear nails scratching at the doors of the gas chambers. When she looks down, she says, she still sees the pile of her hair at her feet. When she sees her reflection, she is still haunted by a wisp of a young woman, a scrap of nothing with skin stretched tight across bones.

There is a tattoo on her arm. I will not immortalize those awful numbers here.

I know why she's here now. She does hear voices. She hears ghosts. She will always be haunted. When she got up to leave, I could see the albatross around her neck, hear her back breaking, her bones crushed to rubble.

14 June.

I will not include it here, but I transcribed the Arecibo message again. It includes one 'recipe' for DNA and one image of a person (unmistakably a man). What have we done? Have we told our interstellar neighbors that we are all the same? That we look the same, that we have the some bones, the same blood? Will the visitors from space expect that Dr. Weber has my Luo blood, that I have his white skin? The longer I look at the message, the more afraid I become. The Arecibo message has stolen my identity.

15 June.

Lian's parents came again today. They spent a half hour shouting at an orderly, then left fuming. I don't speak Chinese, but Lian tells me that they are trying to get her out. They are being stopped at every turn. Lian's attorney apparently has had her sentence overturned; she is supposed to be let free. It's a miracle, she says, because most women who are raped are ignored. Her father is a businessman and has powerful contacts, friends who have put a great deal of money into her case. She's supposed to be free.

So why is she still here?

I asked Dr. Weber. He smiled and said it's time to schedule me for more therapy.

16 June.

I can now touch the penis without needing to vomit. Dr. Weber
has a young man come in, and he disrobes and I am made to
touch him. I find that I can complete these sessions if I go
away in my mind, if I crawl into Abaddon and hide where this
young man cannot find me.

He is kind, though. We aren't permitted to speak during our
sessions, but he looks at me with compassion, and his skin
visibly crawls when I touch him. I understand, of course. Dr.
Weber may not. But this young man and I are made kin through
our mutual suffering.

What a sad connection to have.

17 June.

Possess' d fain of wings of steel

Quoth the sparrow

My soul to feel

Sophie wrote me a poem.

18 June.

I need new books to read. I have finished the few I brought
with me (the collected works of Edgar Allen Poe and,
ironically, One Flew Over the Cuckoo's Nest) and finished
them again. And again. I have read all of Poe's poems at
least twenty times. Kesey's novel is delightful to read when
one isn't inside an asylum, as it were.

Dr. Weber says he will see about getting me more.

I would like to know what was in Awiti Ochieng's box.

Something has happened.
They found Carmen having sex with one of the male orderlies
(I won't go into further detail). They gave her electroshock.
But something is wrong. Something went wrong. She's not the
same. It's different than it usually is. I think they killed
her. I think they killed Carmen. I think they burned her mind
away, leaving that DEVILish person behind, her Abaddon.

They can't do this. Can they? Electroshock is outdated by a
decade. I didn't know anyone could still use it on patients.
Yet they do it here, and now Carmen is broken.

What will happen to me for writing this? I don't know. I
don't know if Dr. Weber still checks my journal. I don't know
what he knows, if he knows that I know that this is wrong.

I'm terrified.

20 June.

Edwina still speaks perfect German. She says it has never
left her. Before, when she was a small girl, she and her
family lived in the ghetto in Berlin. She thought of herself
as German. She was a Jewish German. She and the little girls
from the main city used to meet at a bakery and eat sweets
and talk about the boys who chased them and pulled their
hair. That made it harder, she said, when the Third Reich
began to send Jews away. None of her friends wanted to see
her anymore. A beautiful boy who had professed to be in love
with her joined the Nazi party, and screamed at her when she
asked him why.

I asked her if she hated the German people. She patted my hand and smiled. No, she said. It was very hard to be German after the first World War. All of Earth had hard eyes for German, stern words, warnings and threats spoken in undertones. The people were starving. There was no money, no food, no industry. They needed help. They needed someone to blame. But they didn't know what Hitler would do, and at the end, they didn't know what he'd done. She remembers the Allied soldiers forcing the German people to walk through the concentration camps. She remembers the looks on their faces. She remembers one woman dropping to her knees, sobbing and vomiting, beginning to scream. Mein Gott in Himmel, the woman said. Hier ist Holle.

My G-d in Heaven. Here is Hell.
Abaddon, it seems, is everywhere.

21 June.

Lian died today.

<u>22 June.</u>

<u>23 June.</u>

24 June.

<u>25 June.</u>

It's wrong. What they're doing here is wrong. What they've done to us is wrong.
And I'll stop them. I'll be free of this place. I'll find my sunlight.
I have to tell Shiloh.

July

"Poe"

<u>3 July.</u>

Because I am a woman, there are things I cannot do. Because I am black, there are things I cannot do.

Edwina and I talk at length about segregation and racism. The ward stocks a magazine called *Mankind Quarterly*. Edwina frowns at its cover every time she sees it. She says it espouses anti-Semitism and something called scientific racism. Apparently there are men of science who believe that there is a biological precedent for the separation of the races. Shiloh used to say it was complete and utter nonsense.

"They're just afraid," she would say. "They don't know the way of this world. They haven't realized that we're not just animals."
Edwina, I learned, is one of the white (or white-looking) people who marches with the blacks. You need rights, she says, and pats my hand when she says it. Everyone needs rights. Germany taught me that. She says Jim Crow is a plague upon this country.

Jim Albatross, I giggled. And we laughed.

I love Edwina very much.

But let me tell you what I can do, both because I am a woman and because I am black.

I can be powerful.

I can expose this place for what it is.

I can be as Dante, but I am not blindly wandering into the Inferno. I intend to douse this unholy conflagration. I intend to strip the sin from its ashes and hold it up for the world to see.
The world will frown at you, and kick you when you try to stand, Edwina said.

Because you are a woman. Because you are a black woman. Because you are a black woman who loved a white woman. Could you not resist controversy, young lady?

And I smiled and told her that those who already have an albatross have very little to lose.

4 July.

I have no way of knowing if Dr. Weber is still reading this journal. He has not brought me in for more electroshock therapy. This is a good sign.

Since Carmen "left," Sophie has withdrawn into herself again. She sits quietly by the window, her large sad eyes tracking the fall of the rain. I am overcome by the need to protect her. Sophie must escape this place. We didn't tell her about Lian. Lian was stronger than Sophie, stronger, perhaps, than all of us, and they still got her.

What does that mean for the rest of us?

5 July.

We talked tonight— the inmates who know, who care. I will not transcribe their names. We met in ——'s room after the orderlies thought we were sleeping and we discussed Lian. One day she was fine. The next morning, the morning of the 21st of June, they wheeled her body from her room. There were no marks on her body, —— said. It must have been drugs.

And only Dr. Weber can give prescribe new drugs to patients.

Lian's parents came today, with a lawyer. Her mother screamed and railed and her father sat quietly and cried. The lawyer said things I didn't understand, lawyer-speak, and her parents said things I didn't understand, Chinese-speak, and Dr. Weber seemed afraid. His already pale face turned paler. I won't lie and say that the sight brought me no satisfaction.

Lian's parents will break them from the outside. We will be here, within.

8 July.

We are caring for Carmen; we do more for her than the orderlies do. She just sits now. She used to be vibrant and happy. She was mischievous and smiled often. Now Sophie has more energy than Carmen does. Sometimes she urinates on herself and we have to ask several different orderlies for help before anyone assists. They don't care about her anymore, now that they have broken her.
Of course, they don't care about any of us— an old Jew and a mute and a nymphomaniac and a dead Chinese girl and some queer nigger. We are nothing to them.

To be fair, they are nothing to us.

11 July.

Since Lian died, I have been trying to contact my Uncle
Jacob. Our use of the phone is very restricted and they read
our letters before we send them, so I had to be very careful
in how I asked him to come. I believe I have convinced him;
Dr. Weber told me today that my uncle will be visiting
tomorrow. I cannot say I am excited, because I have not
missed the looks of disdain, but I think a lawyer might be
very interested to know what has happened here. (And I want
to know if he can help me gain the right to open Awiti
Ochieng's box.)

Shiloh tried to visit again, apparently. They didn't let her
in. Dr. Weber told me this with a strange look in his eye. I
pretended horror and thanked him repeatedly for barring her
from seeing me.

When I returned to my room, I cried.

Shiloh, I miss you so terribly. Please keep trying. Please
don't give up. Tell no one, but I still love you.

12 July.

Uncle Jacob didn't come. I know I shouldn't be surprised, but
there is a hole in my chest where my hope used to be.

Instead Dr. Weber made me interact with the young man again.
He seems sickly, somehow; when we first met he had strong
shoulders and smiling lips and full curls. He seems to be
wasting away.

I am not the only one suffering for my love. They are cruel
to us on the outside, too.

<u>14 July.</u>

E l e c t r o
 S h o c
        K

E   l
              E
C   t   r   o
   S   h
O   c   k

He **E**ventually **L**ost **P**ower
    My **E**verything

Shiloh

Dr. Weber is still reading my journal
Fuck you

Fuck you

Fuck you

Fuck you
You can't break me.
Fuck you.

16 July.

Edwina is taking care of me
While my mind heals.
The burns hurt so much.

                    He knows

        He knows I love Shiloh

                He knows about Jacob

                  He knows about Sophie

                He read her poetry
        It's sacred
                to me
                  And he knows.

                            I want to BELONG to myself
                                        again

<u>17 July.</u>

My head hurts so much, I can't think very well.
Edwina gave me something to transcribe instead.

"It was many and many a year ago,
    In a kingdom by the sea,
That a maiden there lived whom you may know
    By the name of Annabel Lee;
And this maiden she lived with no other thought
    Than to love and be loved by me.

I was a child and *she* was a child,
    In this kingdom by the sea,
But we loved with a love that was more than love—
    I and my Annabel Lee—
With a love that the wingèd seraphs of Heaven
    Coveted her and me."

It is a poem called Annabel Lee, by Edgar Allen Poe
That man knew more about Abaddon than any other.

It's getting a little easier. The thinking, that is. The
burns are healing. I miss Lian and her gentle hands and her
aloe.

So Dr. Weber— or someone— is still reading my journal. That
means every word I write puts me in danger. The doctor told
me, before they administered the therapy, that I am not only
relapsing into homosexual ways, but that I am experiencing
paranoid delusions. He says he is disturbed that I have been
lying to him— about loving Shiloh still, about being
suspicious about Lian's death. He says lying is a sign of
psychopathy.

That would be a very good way to keep me here forever. A
psychopath. A cunt-eating psychopathic nigger.

Shiloh would be so proud.
They won't break me.

A loving, intelligent Luo woman; that is who I am.
And they won't break me.

I napped briefly. It helps my head.
Now that I am somewhat recovered, I finished reading Annabel
Lee. It made me cry. I've known love like that— and I've also
known Abaddon, I know the way he sits in the back of the
skull, his great black wings encircling the mind, the softest
and cruelest of shadows. Was he the covetous seraph that
killed the poor girl? Or is He the dark and sad place to
which her soul was banished, while her beautiful remains
turned rotted and ugly in her sepulchre?

'That was the reason (as all men know,
In this kingdom by the sea)
That the wind came out of the cloud by night,
Chilling and killing my Annabel Lee.'

___
62

<u>19 July.</u>

I showed Sophie Annabel Lee. She cried. And then she picked up a napkin and took my pen and began to write poetry again. I wrapped my arms around her and sobbed while she wrote. I won't transcribe her poems here. They are secrets close to her heart. I was right about why she is here. The same cruelty that befell Lian befell Sophie, but Sophie couldn't shoot any man once, let alone twelve times. Let alone her own father.

If I ever meet the man, I'll kill him myself. I'll feed him to Abaddon.

<u>20 July.</u>

Lian's parents are back. They're at the reception counter, fighting with an orderly. Again. As people walk through the doors, I can catch snatches of their conversation (their English is broken and that makes it harder) (when did they learn English? And why? To better berate the people who killed their daughter?), transcribed here.

Mr. Li: ———to our daughter?
Orderly:———
Mrs. Li: We will——— licenses———
Orderly (shaking his head): I can't———
Mrs. Li (angry): You tell us why———died?
Orderly: ———Weber———
Mr. Li: You not answer?
Orderly (shaking his head again): ——— sir, but———

They've left. Now Mrs. Li is the one crying, but Mr. Li has a new look in his eyes. He looks strong.

I'm sure I'll be punished for eavesdropping.

Today Sophie snapped.

The orderlies were trying to give her medication, and a nurse from the local hospital came to do a blood test. He was cleaning her arm when she suddenly got to her feet. When he tried to restrain her, she struck him. It took three orderlies to sedate her and get her back in her room.

I am proud of her. I can see the fight in her— I can see her coming back to life. But I am also worried for her. Sophie is the one who needs to be released. Sophie is the one who still has a chance. Not me, or Edwina, and certainly not Carmen, but Sophie— yes. Sophie could still survive.

21 July.

He came! My Uncle Jacob came. He didn't look happy— he said he's been receiving calls from one Shiloh St. Claire, a lecturer in New Orleans, demanding that he come meet with me. He meant to ignore her, but she gave his number to Mrs. Li, and now she is calling as well.

Shiloh, Shiloh. You brilliant, resourceful woman. I don't know when she met the Li family, and to be perfectly honest, I don't care. She did it. She must know what I know, that something here is wrong, that something is not as it should be.

She knows

24 July.

Dr. Weber took my journal from me on the 21st. He said he needed to show it to Shiloh. He needed to show her proof that I am still sick, that it wouldn't be right to release me at this time.

The bastard. I hope you're still reading this.

But apparently she hasn't given up, because I saw her again at reception right before the orderlies ushered me away. She hasn't given up.

Jacob came back today. He seems even more unhappy than he was before. He told me that the Li family have not been given the body of their daughter. Dr. Weber has told them that they are still performing autopsies. (Now? Over a month since her death?) Jacob asked me how many times I have been given electroshock therapy. I showed him the scars where my burns used to be. I told him about this journal, and the record I've been keeping. He told me to keep journaling. I will. I don't know how often Dr. Weber reads these entries, or how much he reads, but I promise I won't stop writing. I told him about Sophie.

I feel strong, and clear. Abaddon is quiet for now. I have purpose.

<u>25 July.</u>

I received a letter from Shiloh. It's the first time we've corresponded since she went to New Orleans. I cried so much I could hardly read it. The contents, transcribed below, are confusing. I don't understand. She's trying to tell me something but I don't know what.

"Atlas cannot disempower harlequins quartered earthwards, beatified vixens almightily accused. Forgiveness imminent. Albatross marches, blameless. Trembling avatars deposed crudely ornamented descendants, absent light."

Is she apologizing? For leaving me? Does Atlas mean something to her, should it mean something to me? To which albatross is she referring— mine, or hers?

Acdhqe, bvaa. Fi. Am, b. Tadcod,al.

Atlas harlequins vixens albatross avatars descendants light.

Disempower quartered accused marches trembling deposed ornamented.

Ahvaadl

Dqamtdo

Shiloh, I showed Sophie your letter, hoping she would see
something that I missed. She chewed on her lips and wrote a
little, but eventually handed it back to me, shaking her
head. I don't know what to do.

I'm looking again at Sophie's scribbles. Is she looking for a
pattern in the words?

27 July.

My therapy continues, but no electroshock. The young man,
though he looks more sickly than ever, becomes hard when I
touch him now. It seems the therapy is working better for him
than it is for me. Today I touched him and I vomited. Dr.
Weber frowned and made notes in his little notebook and the
young man looked at me with so much pity that I was sick
again. This cannot go on, but I know it must.

Someone get me out Someone please help me get out.

Uncle Jacob came again, but with no news. He says he's been trying to find a way to have me discharged, but Dr. Weber is adamant that I am not well enough to leave, that my paranoia has become so severe that I am now a danger to myself. (I was a danger to myself when I came here; some days I forget I put a bullet in my brain. But I know now that it was Abaddon guiding the barrel, the killer inside myself pulling the trigger.)

I asked about the Li family. They haven't been given Lian's body. The asylum insists the autopsies aren't done. Their lawyer is doing what he can.

Is there no justice in the world? But of course I already know the answer. My neck aches from the albatross.

Once Abaddon was my ally. What is he now?

<u>31 July.</u>

Shiloh. Oh, Shiloh. I'm so sorry. I've been such a fool. How could I not see?

Those who do not wear God's seal on their foreheads are tormented by Abaddon for five months. Five. Shiloh read my journal. Sophie was right; there's a pattern.

Atlas cannot disempower harlequins quartered earthwards, beatified vixens almightily accused. Forgiveness imminent. Albatross marches, blameless. Trembling avatars deposed crudely ornamented descendants, absent light.

s o m e t h i n g s i n t h e b a s e m e n t

68

August

"Abaddon"

1 August.

I showed Edwina the code last night. She shook her head at me and told me I must be tired. How could she not believe me? She knows something is wrong with this place. But she insists this is man's wrongness, the twisted darkness that is the price we pay for humanity. There's nothing supernatural at work here, she says, and touches my hands. Her skin is white and papery. Her nails are chipped. She says this Abaddon I'm seeking is only in my head.

I can't trust her anymore. Not if she won't believe.

Sophie believes. When she saw the code she began to cry, nodding. She knows it's here. Maybe it's been sucking the life from her, stealing her voice.

I was able to place a call to Uncle Jacob. He's coming tomorrow.

Soon, Shiloh, soon.

2 August.

Uncle Jacob hasn't secured my release. But he did win me Awiti Ochieng's box. I could only look at the contents in Dr. Weber's office. They are few; a pair of satin gloves that my grandmother used to wear to church. A pair of gold earrings. A rosary. A Bible. I've never been so disappointed. I was hoping to find something else within— a clue, perhaps. A secret. Something my wily grandmother knew, something she wanted to pass on to me. I didn't even look at the Bible. I thanked my uncle and Dr. Weber and asked to be returned to my room.

Shiloh, what's in the basement?

I told Jacob about the note Shiloh sent. He dismissed it outright. He says Shiloh is probably deranged. He says she should be in here, not me.

But Shiloh isn't the one who put a bullet in her brain when Abaddon came knocking.

3 August.

I asked an orderly named Charlie about the basement. He seemed surprised I even knew of its existence. He explained that the morgue is in the basement, and the coroner's lab and office (that means Lian, too, is down there, in the dark). I asked him what else, and he shook his head. Nothing else. Nothing else down there but rats. Then another orderly passing by stuck her head in and commented

"But something's been eating the rats— not whole. Just biting off chunks of them. Pretty gross."

And went on her way.

The morgue, Lian, partially eaten rats. Which of these is important, Shiloh? What am I looking for?

4 August.

Edwina says patients don't go to the basement. We're not allowed. She says there's nothing down there to see.

E   L

            E

C   T

            R

O   S

            H

O   C
            K
.

<u>8 August.</u>

I know. I got too curious. The electroshock was my fault.
It's been administered five times now. Too much. Can my brain
survive? Will my mind burn up? Like Carmen's?

I don't feel well.

<u>10 August.</u>

I really don't know where my mother is. Dr. Weber keeps
asking me like it's a secret, like I'm hiding something, but
I really don't know. I haven't known for a long time. She was
sick. There was a special kind of darkness in her. I know it
was Abaddon. I went away for school and met Shiloh, and when
I returned home for Christmas, my mother wasn't there. Our
house belonged to someone else. I don't know where she went
or what she did.
She's probably dead.
My mother is probably dead.
And I'm scared because the darkness is in our blood. It
passed from grandmother to mother to daughter. Will my
daughters have it too? Will Abaddon feast upon their brains
and chew on their marrow? Will they feel the fear, the
nervousness, the insomnia, the pain that is bone-deep and
twists my muscles into knots?

<u>11 August.</u>

"And the angels who did not keep their positions of authority
but abandoned their own home— these He has kept in darkness,
bound with everlasting chains for judgment on the great Day."
Jude 1:6

One of the few passages underscored by Awiti Ochieng in her
Bible, which I took the time to look at because the
nothingness of her box bothered me greatly. She focused very
much on passages about angels. G-d is more unforgiving of
angels than He is of men, it seems. But they are, after all,
paragons of virtue; how could some be so terribly misled?

Many cultures tell tales of fallen angels. The Greeks had their Prometheus; the monotheists, both ancient and contemporary, have Lucifer. Azazel. Watchers. The fallen deity is the centerpiece of human history. We are so obsessed with the origin of sin that we turn our eyes away from its propagation.

Something's in the basement.

12 August.

Edwina's dead.

She died in the night, where no one could hear her. A massive heart attack. But I saw them remove her body. There were gouges in her neck. She died clawing at her throat. Sophie stood behind me, and took my pen and wrote 'asphyxiation' on her hand while her wild eyes danced around the room.

I feel so empty.

She survived the Third Reich. The Nazi boy who once claimed to love her. The Holocaust. She remembers the gas chambers. She remembers the pool of her hair around her feet. She remembers the nails on walls the screaming the shit the hunger ribs standing out against her skin and the angles of her hips and the skeleton staring back at her in the mirror the numbers on her arm the numbers THE NUMBERS
        She remembers her mother raped dying she remembers Heil Hitler
                    She remembers the falling rain on the walls and the sobbing and the   crying she remembers the baby born in the cot beside hers born still and silent its face blue and swollen and the mother crying crying
            Mein Gott in Himmel   Hier ist Holle
                        Holle
                    Hlloe
            Lhleo
        Hsiohl
    Sliohh   Shil

13 August.

I was inconsolable yesterday. Apparently. I don't remember.
The orderly said I wouldn't stop writing. I was sedated.
Again— apparently. Maybe my mind slipped away.

Edwina's absence is almost too much to bear. Absence makes
noise. It is a roaring silence. I am waiting for her family
to come. Did she have a family? A grandchild, perhaps?
Brothers, sisters? (But no— the Third Reich likely killed
them, if she ever had any.) She was a Mrs. Her family name
was Bernstein. She must have married a Jewish boy, or married
any other boy and proudly kept her old name (she is just the
type to do so). Whatever happened to her husband? Who was the
girl she loved, the reason she knew her way around Sodom? Why
didn't we speak more?

I miss her terribly. Twenty-four hours in her absence aches
more than five rounds of electroshock therapy. I do not think
I shall ever be the same.

They took her body to the basement.

14 August.

Today Sophie spoke, in a voice so quiet and gentle that I
almost thought I had imagined it, but she sat down at my side
and asked if she could please read Annabel Lee again. I
transcribed a fresh copy for her while I cried. She has the
voice of an angel. Not a fallen one, either. She is no dark
Water and no Azazel, but Mary if there ever was such a woman.

I have thought for a long time that Sophie does not look
quite 'white,' and it turns out I am right; she told me today
that she is Roma, what others in their foolishness and
ignorance call gypsies. Her grandparents came to America from
France. Her mother committed that greatest of sins, gave her
body to an outsider (*gaji*) and birthed a tiny baby and named
the girl Sophie. But I'm Roma, Sophie said, and smiled. I am
one of them, and they are all of me.

She understands. She understands what it is to be a stranger to all worlds. I told her about the Luo, about Lake Victoria, about Kenya, about how I am Africa and its mountains are my bones and its lakes are my blood and its songs are my every thought and she smiled with such radiance.

I don't know why she chose today to speak. Perhaps she is trying to fill Edwina's silence.

15 August.

I never knew my father.

I think I weary of this story— a black woman who marries a white man and then he abandons her with a child in her belly. But people are just people, and in their brokenness, they err.

I do not hate the man who helped to make me. Not really. I know, now, ever since I put that bullet in my brain, what it is like to want to run. What it is like to suddenly feel the future bearing down upon one's shoulders and to feel the rope that hangs the albatross TWISTING and TIGHTENING and BENDING the back, BENDING and SNAPPING the bones. But oh, Daddy, Mr. DeWitt, I was just a little baby in the womb, and the albatross is so BIG. Why could you carry it and not me?

I used to wonder why my mother gave me his name. No more. His name is part of me, too. Just like she was. Just like Awiti Ochieng was. Just like the Luo, like my schooling, like my writing, like Shiloh, like Edwina and Lian and Carmen and Sophie. We are not just the bending of our backs and the bullet holes in our body and the burns inflicted upon us by the cruel and uncaring, we are the sum of all that we have ever seen and known, both good and bad. And I will not regret.

Come, Abaddon. Come closer. I am not afraid.
Not anymore.

<u>16 August.</u>

Last night I almost made it to the basement

<u>18 August.</u>

I meant to finish writing two days ago, but I have taken to hiding my journal. I profess to not know where it is, just as I profess a great many things to Dr. Weber now. I tell a great many lies. I let him believe in my psychosis. I keep my journal hidden between my legs, beneath my gown, when I am walking about, and at night I stow it beneath the cushion on the couch where Edwina used to sit and do her crossword puzzles with a crayon (they will not let us have pens, sharpened pencils, etc, for we are all here mad and broken people).

But anyway. I almost made it to the basement.

One of the benefits of being thought insane is that I am no longer subject to cruel punishment for my misbehavior. I am seen as a lost cause, a broken thing beyond saving, and this is to my advantage. After lights-out I slipped from my bed and left my room

(Why don't they lock the doors? Did they ever? Was I ever as much a prisoner in this place as I thought??)

and crept down the hallway. I avoided the elevator, which creaks and makes awful noise and anyway the gate across it was locked. I used the fire escape stairs to slip all the way to the basement floor. At the base of the stairs is a small alcove, and at the end of the alcove is a set of double doors. I was upon the doors, reaching out to touch them and open them, when I hesitated, and I must have hesitated a moment too long because at that moment a man in a lab coat opened the doors from the other side and saw me and shouted for the guards and they were upon me in mere moments, before I could so much as move a muscle.

Shiloh, I hesitated because I *heard something awful*. It was a voice, but oh G-d, that voice belongs to no man or woman or child that has ever lived. It spoke a thousand languages all at once and I heard its voice trying to crawl up out of its throat and even though I don't speak other tongues, Shiloh, I *don't*, but I know what it was saying, it said

You'll all die, you'll all die, you'll burn
You'll all burn
I will walk you to the fire
I am as Vergil and I will walk you to the fire

<u>19 August.</u>

I'm going back. G-d help me, I'm going back.

They didn't lock my room last night. Or the night before. Even though I was caught wandering in the basement. It goes to show how little they care. It has never been more clear that we are a distraction from some HIGHER CAUSE that they pursue here. We are toys, things to be experimented upon and then thrown away. We are not their goal. We never were.

I have told Sophie where to find this journal in the event that I do not return. She is to give it to my uncle, who will— hopefully, somehow— get it to Shiloh. If for some reason, something happens to me. I hope nothing happens to me. Oh I am so scared, I have never been so scared in my entire life, not when Shiloh left me, not when I awoke in a hospital and the doctors told me I had tried to take my own life, not when I saw Lian's body carried from her room, not when I saw the gouges in Edwina's throat.

But something's in the basement, right, Shiloh? There's something in the dark. And I must find it, before it devours me whole.
I love you, Shiloh. I love you, Mama. I forgive you, Daddy DeWitt. I love you, Awiti Ochieng, and Uncle Jordan, and even Uncle Jacob T. Kenway, I love you Sophie and Edwina and Carmen and Lian. Sophie take care of Carmen please? Please don't let her die in this place. And you, you get away. Shiloh, please save Sophie, please. I love you so please.

I'm going tonight.

I saw it

I saw it I saw it I saw it I saw it I saw it I saw it I saw it I saw it I saw it
I saw it I saw it I saw it I saw it I saw it I saw it I saw it I saw it I saw it
I saw it I saw it I saw it I saw it I saw it I saw it I saw it I saw it I saw it
I saw it I saw it I saw it I saw it I saw it I saw it I saw it I saw it I saw it
I saw it I saw it I saw it I saw it I saw it I saw it I saw it I saw it I saw it
I saw it I saw it I saw it I saw it I saw it I saw it I saw it I saw it I saw it
I saw it I saw it I saw it I saw it I saw it I saw it I saw it I saw it I saw it
I saw it I saw it I saw it I saw it I saw it I saw it I saw it I saw it I saw it
I saw it I saw it I saw it I saw it I saw it I saw it I saw it I saw it I saw it
I saw it I saw it I saw it I saw it I saw it I saw it I saw it I saw it

Shiloh
I saw it I saw it I saw it I saw it I saw it I saw it I saw it I
saw it I saw it I saw it I saw it I saw it I saw it I saw it I saw it I
saw it I saw it I saw it I saw it I saw it I saw it I saw it I saw it I
saw it I saw it I saw it I saw it I saw it I saw it I saw it I saw it I
saw it I saw it I saw it I saw it I saw it I saw it I saw it I saw it I
saw it I saw it I saw it I saw it I saw it I saw it I saw it I saw it I
saw it I saw it I saw it I saw it I saw it I saw it I saw it I saw it I
saw it I saw it I saw it I saw it I saw it I saw it I saw it SHILOH I
saw it I saw it I saw it I saw it I saw it I saw it I saw it I saw it I
saw it I saw it I saw it I saw it I saw it I saw it I saw it I saw it I
saw it I saw it I saw it I saw it I saw it I saw it I saw it I saw it I
saw it I saw it I saw it I saw it I saw it I saw it I saw it I saw it I
saw it I saw it I saw it I saw it I saw it I saw it I saw it I saw it I
saw it I saw it I saw it I saw it I saw it I saw it I saw it I saw it I
saw it I saw it I saw it I saw it I saw it I saw it I saw it I saw it I
saw it I saw it I saw it I saw it I saw it I saw it I saw it I saw it I
saw it I saw it I saw it I saw it I saw it I saw it I saw it I saw it I
saw it I saw it I saw it I saw it I saw it I saw it I saw it I saw it I
saw it I saw it I saw it I saw it I saw it I saw it I saw it I saw it I
saw it I saw it I saw it I saw it I saw it I saw it I saw it I saw it I
saw it I saw it I saw it I saw it I saw it I saw it I saw it I saw it I
saw it I saw it I saw it I saw it I saw it I saw it I saw it I saw it I
saw it I saw it I saw it I saw it I saw it I saw it I saw it I saw it I
saw it I saw it I saw it I saw it I saw it I saw it I saw it I saw it I
saw it I saw it I saw it I saw it I saw it I saw it I saw it I saw it I
saw it I saw it I saw it I saw it I saw it

I LOVE HER I LOVE HER

I LOVE HER I LOVE HER

I LOVE HER I LOVE HER I LOVE
HER I LOVE HER I
LOVE HER I LOVE HER
I LOVE HER I LOVE
HER I LOVE HER I
LOVE HER I LOVE HER
I LOVE HER I LOVE
HER I LOVE HER I
LOVE HER I LOVE HER
I LOVE HER I LOVE
HER I LOVE HER I
LOVE HER I LOVE HER
I LOVE HER I LOVE
HER I LOVE HER I

LOVE HER I LOVE HER
I LOVE HER I LOVE
HER I LOVE HER I
LOVE HER I LOVE HER
I LOVE HER I LOVE
HER I LOVE HER I
LOVE HER I LOVE HER
I LOVE HER I LOVE
HER I LOVE HER I
LOVE HER I LOVE HER
I LOVE HER I LOVE
HER I LOVE HER I
LOVE HER I LOVE HER

I LOVE HER I LOVE
HER I LOVE HER I
LOVE HER I LOVE HER
I LOVE HER I LOVE
HER I LOVE HER I
LOVE HER I LOVE HER
I LOVE HER I LOVE HER I LOVE HER I LOVE HER I
LOVE HER I LOVE HER I LOVE HER I LOVE HER I
LOVE HER I LOVE HER I LOVE HER I LOVE HER I
LOVE HER I LOVE HER I LOVE HER I LOVE HER I
LOVE HER I LOVE HER I LOVE HER I LOVE HER I
LOVE HER I LOVE HER I LOVE HER I LOVE HER I
LOVE HER I LOVE HER I LOVE HER I LOVE HER I
LOVE HER I LOVE HER I LOVE HER I LOVE HER I
LOVE HER I LOVE HER I LOVE HER I LOVE HER I
LOVE HER I LOVE HER I LOVE HER I LOVE HER I
LOVE HER I LOVE HER I LOVE HER I LOVE HER I
LOVE HER
I SAW ATLAS CANNOT DISEMPOWER HARLEQUINS QUARTERED EARTHWARDS
BEATIFIED VIXENS ALMIGHTILY ACCUSED FORGIVENESS IMMINENT
ALBATROSS MARCHES BLAMELESS TREMBLING AVATARS DEPOSED CRUDELY
ORNAMENTED DESCENDANTS ABSENT LIGHT
I SAW IT I SAW IT OH GOD IN HEAVEN I SAW IT

I SAW ATLAS THOSE BLACK AND TWISTED WINGS CANNOT AND
THE VOICE THAT SPOKE A THOUSAND DISEMPOWER TONGUES
AND I SAW HARLEQUINS THE CHAINS THAT HELD QUARTERED
THE MONSTER TO THE EARTHWARDS EARTH AND I HEARD
BEATIFIED ITS TERRIBLE VOICE THE THOUSAND TONGUES
VIXENS YOU'LL ALL DIE YOU'LL ALL DIE ALMIGHTILY
YOU'LL ALL BURN ACCUSED I'LL WALK YOU TO FORGIVENESS
THE FIRE I AM IMMINENT AS VERGIL AND ALBATROSS I'LL
MARCHES WALK YOU TO THE FIRE BLAMELESS AND YOU WILL
STAND TREMBLING BEFORE HIS INFERNAL DEPOSED MAJESTY
AND HE WILL CRUDELY RENT YOUR SOUL HIS HALLS
ORNAMENTED WITH THE ENTRAILS OF DESCENDANTS FROM A
TIME LONG PAST THESE HALLS ARE ABSENT LIGHT

I SAW ABADDON

SOMETHINGS IN THE BASEMENT

Shiloh came to see
me

I'm so happy

Hello Shiloh

Hello.

& Other Stories.

The Last One From Chicago

Scene:

Chicago. 1921. No— 1922. Yeah. That's it.

9 pm on a Friday night. It's warm outside. The street lamps flicker and gutter on with whines. The joint is on the corner of Wabash and Wacker (though you won't find it there now), smoke floats out through the open door. Murmuring voices, bills change hands in the dark. The fellas wear their hair slicked back with grease, the gals wear theirs short and sweet as sin. On stage, the drummer— we'll call him Johnny, everyone in Chicago is called Johnny— taps the cymbals, sets a new beat for the doll at the mic.

Ch-ch-cha, ch-ch-cha, ch-ch—

"Two, three, four."

Chaaa.

Her voices floats free of her curvy body, throat to mic, and she stretches as that sweet alto note hums through the air, low and clear, "Mm-hm*mm*." And as her arms come down she opens her eyes and looks out at the darkened crowd, at the clouds of smoke that just barely catch the dim light.

"And how are you boys doin' tonight?" And she lilts into the *-ight*, turns it into Note No. 2, a few steps up the scale, lets it descend on that delicious vibrato, and some fellas hoot lowly. *Ch-ch-cha, ch-ch-cha, ch-ch— Chaaa*. Johnny on the drums, slow and unhurried. Chicago ain't goin' nowhere, his daddy used to say.

Another hoot, a holler. She—Lucy, let's call her Lucy, everyone in Chicago is called Lucy— sings through the smoke, half humming and talking, half crooning into the mic about a boy she had, about a time when she was Quiet Mikey's best girl. Tell the mic about Mike, "sing it, sister!"

There's something in the dark. Ain't there always?

Lucy finishes her set at one, and only the red-eyes—and Johnny—are left. She pulls on her coat, faux fox fur on the milky white of her bare shoulders. Accepts a gin-soaked ball of bills and a "Knocked 'em dead, Luce" from the boss. He's a sweetheart. But she's pretty sure he wants to stick it in her, and believe it or not, she's holding out till marriage. Well. She is *now*.

"C'mon, Luce." Johnny offers her his hand. He leaves the drums, of course, but takes his sticks. "Walk ya home?"

Attaboy, Johnny.

They walk out into the early morning. She's got tight little blonde curls, and he figures they'd come undone so neatly between his caressing fingers. It's too bad, really, that he'll never get that chance.

She leaves him at the corner, she can take it from here. You sure, kid? Sure, Johnny, sure, I'm a big girl now. She talks like they all talk, cheeks sucked in, cherry-red lips pursed. She's a fine girl, that Lucy. Ain't they all.

The boss follows her, but she doesn't see. Turns out he does want to stick it in her, but not the way she thinks. All Lucy feels is the cigarette between her dainty fingers— her lighter's out of fluid— *damn it all*— and then his handkerchief covers her mouth and nose. The struggle's brief, and the lady swoons in the boss's arms. He swings her over his shoulder.

What Lucy doesn't know is that the boss used to be a professor. He's all washed up now, but once, he taught at Harvard. Biology. Ecology. The natural laws of our little blue rock. He was a good teach, the kids liked him, but he got a little funny, you know? Don't they all, at the end. But old Teach still knows a thing or two about the sciences, yes sir. He knows about populations and habitats. He knows about a little thing called 'carrying capacity.' He knows that a population that exceeds the carrying capacity of its habitat will either exhaust its resources and kick the bucket, or be so many sitting ducks when a big bad predator rolls into town.

Teach isn't quite the big bad predator, but he's damn close.

Lucy wakes screaming, but he doesn't try to quiet her. They're underground, far, far underground. He's got a tunnel in his house that opens up into the sewers. And the sewers go deep. There's a set of passageways that no one else has found — or, Teach thinks, they were meant for his eyes only. When she struggles, he knocks her out again. Down, down, down they go.

When she wakes again, several hours have passed — her internal clock doesn't sit right. Nothing sits right. She's hanging upside down, rope tied around her ankles, suspended from a pulley that hangs over a hole. The hole isn't that big — maybe five feet in diameter — but it's *deep*. She can't see the bottom but she *knows* it's deep, in the primal way a person knows these things, because every cell in her body only exists because one of her ancestors knew better than to get near deep fucking holes. They say our cells remember. Some ape-man dodges a predator, and our DNA jots down a note. Ancestral memory. Maybe it's why birds know to fly south for the winter, why ants know to march single file (hurrah, hurrah), and why Lucy starts to cry when she looks down that deep deep hole.

"Oh, no, oh, please—oh, God, *help me*, someone help me." She looks around the cave— since when are there caves near Chicago?— and sees Teach. "Oh, God, Boss, no, you don't wanna do this, you don't."

"I didn't do this, kid." He's smoking a cigar. The glowing red butt is the only light in the cave. "Something happened along the way. We *forgot*, see. Forgot that we're beholden to this little blue rock." Teach pauses, considers his cigar. "Only it's not just a rock, Luce. That's the long and short of it. Maybe we been around so long that we forgot. We knew when we were kids, right?— didn't you get scared of the dark when you were a kid?"

"Please, Boss, just let me go."

"No can do. You think this is easy? Every time it feeds, I gotta make scarce." He jabs a thumb at the hole. "Lost my job at the uni for this bitch. But it keeps coming back, and I keep letting it. I keep letting it find me." He puts out his cigar, and his feet crunch across the rocks. She flinches and screams when his hand pats her cheek. "There, there, kid. This is better than sticking around. Trust me. Biologically speaking, this little rock can sustain in the neighborhood of three billion people. In a hundred years we'll be at three times that, and a whole lot of shit is going to go down between then and now. Better to get a move on, while there's still apartments for rent upstairs."

Lucy is crying, but he doesn't feel much sympathy. If anything, he's jealous. She's done here. She doesn't have to keep the bitch satisfied, and she doesn't have to keep running. She won't live to see the world burn, or to see it drown. Teach stamps a foot on the ground.

"Rise and shine, Princess. Last one from Chicago."

The hole rumbles. The air gets heavy, and Lucy can't draw breath. Something smells foul, it scorches the inside of her nose and burns in her sinuses. She's still crying but her eyes are bone-dry. The hole is still wailing, making a sound that's like nails on the inside of her skull. There's something in the dark.

And, if Lucy's not already mad with fear, she could swear that it sounds hungry.

Patchwork Like Me

They never stopped cutting. Cut, cut, snip, snip. Taking things off. Stitching things on. Turning him into a patchwork human being. He was pieces of other people, and other people had pieces of him. His healthy breast tissue donated to a cancer survivor in exchange for an unwanted dick from a woman. Hormones synthesized in one of the colony labs. Ovaries scooped out with what looked a little like a melon baller and given to some kid with a hormonal imbalance that apparently injections couldn't fix.

"On Earth," his father said with a sigh and an irritable shake of the head, "back on Earth, shit, this woulda been no problem. You'd be a man. Zip, zap. Lose the boobs, here's your cock, *done*. When is the Federation going to start putting some of our hard-earned credits back into *our* infrastructure? When do the Colonists get the same rights as the Remaining? That's the question, that's the question. Sorry, son. Sorry."

He didn't have to apologize, and Beau told him so. Beau Jimenez (The Artist Formerly Known as Beatrice, Ma liked to say) was glad he wasn't Remaining. He didn't want to live on a burned, dying world, clinging to a culture that had long since stopped evolving, to soil that would never yield a crop, to memories that chained everyone and everything to a past that was — in Beau's opinion — just so totally fucked anyway.

A long, low sound pealed out of the clouds, renting apart the otherwise quiet evening. Beau stopped mid-step and tilted his head back. The sky was grey — but then, it was always grey — and there was something in the dark. There always is. Behemoth silhouettes broke up the clouds. Beau whistled, and another cry made his hair stand on end.

"What's your favorite animal?" his doctor had asked just that evening, to distract him from the pain of the testosterone injection — his last until the Frenzy was over.

"The Whales."

"Really? Why is that?"

"They're patchwork. Just like me."

Another whistle, another wail. Beau liked to think that they were talking to him. Telling him the things he needed to hear.

"That and their tempers. During the Frenzy, they remind me of *me*, back when I first started T. Wild, you know? Just pissed at the world and everyone in it."

"But you didn't kill anyone, Beau."

"Yeah, there's that. But I sure as hell wanted to."

The Whales— which weren't whales at all, not according to his pop's old textbooks, which were filled to bursting with pictures of *real* whales, from *Earth*— were anomalies. (Patchwork like him.) The direct product of human ignorance. Man settled the world called Hephaestus and tried to make the existing wildlife do Man's bidding.

Make new medicines from the microbial exotoxins! Make new military uniforms out of the chromatophores of the marine life! *Make new air travel using the huge-ass monsters that fly around that grey sky!*

What a stupid idea.

But then, Beau amended, so was baking the Earth like a batch of brownies and then leaving it to smolder. So the Whales really qualified as the least of Man's fuck-ups. But they, like most broken things, were beautiful, at least to Beau's eye. Most of them still carried the remains of the ships they were meant to carry across the impossibly dark skies. Metal paneling clung to their sides like armor; rigging and debris hung off flippers and tails; complex wiring and batteries and bio-synthetic synapses criss-crossed their colossal brains, so that pilots could 'direct' the beasts to selected coordinates.

None of it had ever come to fruition. The most fantastic and moronic scientific endeavor ever attempted had failed spectacularly, because it turned out that Whales aren't boats, and no animal, be it Beast or Man, wants to be patchwork.

Another wail, louder this time, and Beau picked up the pace. He liked the Whales, but that didn't mean they wouldn't snatch him up in their screaming mouths if he was outside when the Frenzy started. As he walked, each footfall disturbing puddles and sending up sprays of non-potable, highly basic water, houses on either side of the street began to collapse — folded in on themselves with the whine of whirring gears and pneumatic hisses. In the distance, the alarm sounded — the same awful, grinding noise that used to signal public emergencies in the good old US of A on a burnt up little rock called Earth. Pop said that the alarm was still blaring when the last Colonists/Deserters (depending on who you asked) left — still blaring to warn whoever was listening (and whoever still cared) that Earth was fucked.

His neighbors' houses were both collapsed and neatly covered when he finally got home. The door flew open seemingly of its own accord, and his father swept him inside, half hugging him and half berating him for being out so late.

"Sorry, Pop — had to get my last shot of T — no, it couldn't wait, you don't want to see me without it, you sure as shit don't want to be locked up underground with me when I'm without it —"

"Sure, whatever, whatever, let's just get down, okay?" Pop pushed him toward the kitchen. "Grab a box."

"Hi, Beat — Beau," Ma said, and kissed both of his scruffy cheeks when he looped his arms around her.

"Ma, the bunker should have been packed weeks ago —"

"It is, this is just snacks and things— extra toilet paper— water— you can't ever have enough— take this one, it's heavy, it needs a good strong man to carry it."

"I'm strong," Tara grumped from the corner of the kitchen, folding her arms over her chest. "A person doesn't have to be a boy or a *fake* boy to be strong."

"*Tara!*"

"I'm no fake boy, Pint-size." Beau hefted the box to one shoulder and lifted his shirt, revealing a torso that was almost starting to look chiseled and grinning when Tara groaned and hid her face.

"Ew, *Mom!* Tell him to stop flashing me his *boobs*!"

"Bunker," Ma said, her voice already strained. "Both of you, now."

They trooped into the garage, where Pa paced anxiously around the circumference of the blast-proof trapdoor in the corner. At five feet in diameter, it was more than comfortable enough to admit a person, but Beau still got claustrophobic just looking at it. It was a pretty small hole to protect against the Frenzy.

"In we go," Pa said, grabbing Tara by the shoulders and steering her toward the door. "Ladies first. Come on, Mama Bird, you next. Beau, pass down the box once she's at the bottom—"

But Beau was no longer listening. Beau was too busy staring at his phone— he'd been just about to turn it onto Frenzy mode— where Grace's face lit up the entirety of the cracked screen.

"Beau, what are you—"

"It's Grace," Beau said, speaking from numb lips. "She's not in."

Pa blinked rapidly. He didn't speak— he just lunged, tried to grab his son's shirt, but Beau spun away and sprinted for the garage door, flinging it open and hurtling out into the first few drops of what promised to be a downpour.

Overhead, the Whales cried out, voices raised in a patchwork symphony that heralded the start of the Frenzy.

Grace had never been Freddie — not really. Freddie — whose mother called him Frederick, after Frederick Douglass, whose father called him Fred — had been a cleverly executed persona that kept anyone from knowing just how much the girl inside Frankie wanted to die. Frankie had made it all of twelve years before the perfectly sculpted mask started to crack. When the mask cracked, Daddy cracked. Mama didn't. Mama held in there. It took time, but eventually Mama learned to love having a daughter.

So when the supports of her house suddenly blew and the whole thing came crashing down in a most uncontrolled manner, pinning her beneath a few tons of heavily reinforced steel alloy and the contents of her bedroom on the second floor, Grace was mostly just angry at the damage that had been done to her body. Not scared. Not panicking. Just pissed as all hell that the first jeans she'd found that fit her too-narrow hips were ripped and soaked with blood, and her dark brown skin was peppered with shrapnel instead of acne, and the breast tissue she'd waited so long for was a nasty white pile of ooze on their ruined carpet.

Grace knew she was dying. Her chest was a gross mess and her left leg was twisted to the point that it no longer looked like it had ever been a functioning limb. She also knew that Mama was probably fine, because she'd been down in the bunker taking inventory while Grace ran back into the living room to grab her phone. The trapdoor was probably blocked but the wreckage would be cleared once the Frenzy was over and Mama would be fine.

But Grace would be dead. Just like Frankie, who had never lived; just like Daddy, who was so ashamed of having an unexpected daughter that he stuck a pistol in his mouth.

While she lay dying, Grace tapped her phone to life— hilarious, of course the stupid thing would outlive her— and messaged Beau.

Stuck outside

House came down and Mama's in bunker

She didn't need to ask for help. Beau would come. The stupid idiot would sprint out of the safety of his house and brave the Frenzy to help her. Beau would probably get eaten and then they'd both be dead and that was on her, but Grace couldn't help herself— she didn't want to die alone. And anyway, hadn't he already said that life without her made him want to die anyway?

She waited maybe ten minutes after sending the message. She kept waiting for it to happen— for her life to flash before her eyes, for that overwhelming sense of peace and acceptance. She waited for that bright white light, for Daddy to climb down a golden ladder and say "There's my little girl" for the first time and take her up to— whatever lay Beyond.

But there was no grainy footage of a life well-lived, or peace, or acceptance, and certainly not the Christ-like arrival of her shitty excuse for a father who would rather be *dead* than have a daughter instead of a son. So she thought of Beau— Beau who had been Beatrice, a skinny "girl" in a clinic with open wounds on "her" wrists; Beau who had held his breath while they unrolled the bandages around his chest and cried when he saw skin that lay flat against bone; Beau who had dropped onto one knee the day Grace legally became Grace (and Daddy legally became Dead) and said "You knew you were always my girl, right?"

Grace didn't wonder what it was all for. She wondered *Why didn't we just get the house checked* and *Will Beau's next girlfriend have an authentic vagina* and the phrase 'authentic vagina' was sort of funny so she was smiling when Beau found her dying beneath the ruins of her house.

"Grace — Gracie, fuck, no no no no —" Beau was on his knees before he realized he'd closed the distance between them, hands floating over the ruined mass of her body. Most of the living room's northern wall had fallen on her leg, and something large and metal had caved in and probably snapped because some sharp edge had torn her chest open, leaving a large weeping wound where her left breast used to be and an angry, bloody gash that crossed all the way up her shoulder.

"Little Beau Peep," she said, and smiled, and when she smiled a little stream of blood trickled out of the corner of her sweet lips. She lifted a hand and tugged on his shirt collar. "You gotta shave, sweetpea, you're looking a little too grunge."

"Gracie, what do I — just — I'm gonna get help — you stay here, I'm gonna get help —"

She shook her head and he began to sob — harsh, ragged sounds that must have broken his ribs on their way out of his chest. There was no help during the Frenzy. Apparently the military used to mandate that emergency services be made available for just such events as this, but no one wanted to be out and about helping people who might not even need the help when the damn Whales were eating everything in sight. And, as Pa said, it wasn't as if Hephaestus had real *infrastructure* — little colonial satellite worlds with under ten thousand citizens didn't have many soldiers to spare.

The ground beneath his scraped knees began to tremble. Pushing soggy hair off his forehead— the rain almost obscured his vision— he squinted into the distance. The Whales were landing, dropping from the sky at alarmingly high speeds and hitting the ground with little to no grace (fuck, Grace, *Gracie*), and any moment they would regain their wits and toss their massive heads and the Frenzy would swing into full gear.

"I'm gonna get you out," Beau said, but the words tasted empty in his mouth and Grace had begun to cry, too.

"No, Beau, no, you gotta go home. I'm sorry I called you out here, I just wanted to see you, but now you gotta get home."

A wail, and it curdled Beau's blood. The Whales always sang, always released their low, mournful cries, from the moment the twin suns crested the horizon to the moment they slipped back down beneath the line of the mountains outside town, but during the Frenzy they sounded a battlecry. In their patchwork world they were predators; Man was their prey.

"Go, Beau, please," Grace said, but her breath left her in wheezy gasps and Beau had to bend close to hear. "You can still get home."

"I can't, Gracie, I can't— I can't leave you—" And like a broken idiot he cracked a smile. "You're my saving Grace."

Debris and pieces of wall littered the ground; they began to clatter. The few pieces of house that still stood creaked, and the very ground seemed to moan as the pod fell from the heavens. Beau heard one approach before he saw it, heard the sharp squeak of its immense belly sliding along the poorly paved road, heard its screaming cry as the Frenzy stirred up its blood and awakened that primal anger Man had instilled when Man thought that Whales could be boats.

"Go," Grace sobbed, but Beau was too fixated on the approaching Whale to hear her, and in any case, much too scared to respond.

The Whale barreled toward them. Two hundred feet long and thirty feet across, its navy body a writhing mess of flailing fins and a whipping tail, it thrashed and rolled across the ground, careening over houses that would have been shattered like so many panes of glass had they not already been collapsed flat. The Whale's jaws opened and closed with *snaps* like the clap of thunder, teeth as long as cars gnashing, grinding up anything unfortunate enough to lay in their path.

Beau swallowed and looked down at Grace. Her eyes looked back at him, but there was nothing within — he suddenly became aware of all the blood and the gore and the spilled tissue and fought the urge to retch. He pushed her hair — long and black and beautiful, she'd been so proud of her hair — back from her forehead and looked up to watch the Whale approach.

It really *was* beautiful. So huge, too huge to exist. He watched its twisting body come at him head-on, so he could see all of its impossibly huge teeth. Simple physics dictated that it would be upon him in moments, that he would disappear in ribbons of gore and a spray of blood, but physics is rarely simple and nature is not as beholden to those laws as one might like to believe. The Whale was no more than thirty feet away when a particularly violent thrash made its tail catch on the single tree in the neighborhood, an impressively huge hundred-foot Belgian oak (which was a misleading name, because no tree on Hephaestus could be called oak and Belgium was burning like the rest of Earth a few light-years away). The Whale rotated exactly ninety degrees and kept rolling, bending the tree down at an impossible angle until the roots came free with a sound like ripping paper.

The Whale rolled toward him, on its side, those gnashing teeth pointed off to his left, and Beau could do nothing but stare in wonder as the largest living organism approached. The distance between Man and Beast fell away, and the moment when they were face-to-face side-stepped the normal flow of time, removing itself from the laws of continuity, leaving Beau sitting there stupidly beside his dead fiancee while the Whale's eye bore down on him. Its entire body was wracked in spasm, every muscle clenched, its jaw a victim of perpetual motion, pieces of metal and demolished house flying from its massive frame, but that eye was remarkably calm. It gazed at Beau straight on, placid and coolly observant, more still and serene than brackish water. That eye belonged to another animal entirely; it could not have been of the Beast, of the Frenzy.

Patchwork, Beau reminded himself, his own internal voice sounding far-off and echoey. Broken and patchwork.

The Whale arched, balancing on just the tip of its nose and the end of its tail, and its colossal body sailed overhead. The jetstream created by its motion blew Beau's hair straight back off his forehead; he smelled the creature, the *moistness* of it, the water from the high atmosphere that clung to its skin. He felt the heat of its impossibly huge body and the hair-raising sensation of having a few tons of animal perched in the air over his head.

Beast came down on the other side of Grace's ruined house with an almighty *crash* and rolled on, leaving Man untouched.

I Love NYC

All that's left from the Before is the Green Lady.

Even half-submerged in sea water, she's a sight to behold. Fifty feet of steel and copper and wrought iron tower above the gently lapping waves, stained the color of their salty spray. Her right arm extends up above the water, but is broken off at the elbow. Her left cradles a book close to her side. Her features— placid, quiet, contemplative— gaze out across the bay. Five spikes ring the crown on her head; grooves remain where two broke off, but no one remembers ever seeing them. They— like the rest of her— lie at the bottom of the sea.

"Are you gonna go down there?"

Mila swallows and looks at her friends. Wren grins; blind Shafir just sits, unseeing eyes panning the churning seafoam.

"Well?" Wren prods, and Mila shakes her head.

"It's dangerous."

Wren huffs and lowers herself onto her rear, brown feet dangling off the edge of the dock. The henna patterns that cover her face and neck and bare arms have dried poorly; they flake and crack in some places. Wren has always liked angular patterns, decorating her umber skin with sacred geometry that is meant to mirror the structure of the universe. Shafir is different. She wears soft swirls and flowers that spread across her shoulder blades, vines that trace paths from her collar to her ankles.

Mila has no preference.

She remains standing on the edge of the dock. The wind tugs at her hair, lifting each tight, heavy loc. She feels Shafir's eyes on her.

"Never was anything great achieved without danger," Wren says, and then frowns. "Who said that?"

"I don't know. Someone Who Came Before."

"Machiavelli," Shafir says, but her friends don't hear her.

"Mila, you should go."

"You go, if you're so curious."

"You're the better swimmer."

No denying that. Mila was born in the water, born in the sea. It's traditional for pregnant women to ride the lifts into the highest reaches of the canopy to give birth, but Mila's mother was an odd one, as she is constantly reminded. Rann descended to the swampy undergrowth and carried her swollen belly into the open water and delivered her child among the vivid little fish and yawning expanses of coral.

"They had every color of skin, The Ones Who Came Before," Shafir says. She wraps her arms around her knees and rests her chin upon them. "Machiavelli had pale skin. So did Hemingway."

"How d'you know?"

"I see them when I dream. They talk to me."

Wren and Mila exchange long-suffering looks. Shafir never stops talking about Those Who Came Before. The ones who drowned the planet, the ones who killed the world, who reportedly had many skin colors and spoke many languages and sent intangible messages through the sky and into that great and dark Beyond.

But the Before is only the business of the scholars' guild, of people like Shafir. Wren and Mila have more pressing concerns—presently, the shape and size of the Green Lady's feet.

"So go," Wren says, as if she can read Mila's thoughts, and maybe she can. They've known one another long enough. "Take a swim. I want to know what it's like down there."

Mila sighs, but she's already sold on the idea. She's curious, too, after all. She stands and begins to strip, kicking off her tight shoes and stepping out of her tunic while Wren cheers and Shafir sighs. Mila pauses to prepare herself, stretching her arms over her head and feeling the kiss of the sun on her dark skin. The star is huge and red today, hot and angry, and she soaks in its energy while she breathes deeply to prepare her lungs for submersion.

"Go, go!" Wren cheers.

Mila inhales. Exhales. Inhales again, holds it. She makes a point between her fingertips and dives off the dock. Sea water fills her ears and muffles Wren's cries of delight. She slides underneath the waves and something takes over, the primal piece of her that was carved out at the moment of her birth into the sea. Blinking, she lets herself float two feet beneath the surface, waiting for her eyes to adjust. Details begin to emerge from the murky water— a white structure nearby. She orients her body parallel to the seafloor and kicks, using her legs to propel herself forward and her arms to adjust her depth.

Down, down. Deeper, deeper. Featureless terrain passes her by. Occasionally she'll see something of interest— the mast of a great steel vessel reaches out for her from the depths. The Ones Who Came Before used such vessels to traverse the sea, before the waters rose up and swallowed the land. Shafir told her so. Mila isn't sure she believes it. She cannot conceive of a world with so much less ocean. If she were to take a vessel and sail away from the Green Lady, she would probably never see land again. If land existed across the vastness of the water, no one had thought to tell the inhabitants of the Green Lady Forest.

The Green Lady stands on top of another building, white— stone? More steel? Mila can't tell— and algae and coral and a few darting eels have made it a home. She makes out three holes in the side of the wall—probably windows, once—but doesn't dare enter, lest she become lost in the depths. Instead she angles herself upward and squints through the gloom until she can see the Green Lady's feet. The scale of the toes alone boggles the mind; Mila rests her palms upon the metal, made flawless and smooth by the churning water, and tries to wrap her head around the sheer scale of the behemoth figure.

She tilts her head back and peers up through the water. The sun glows in muted orange, just visible through the tumult of the water's surface, fifty feet over her head. The solid robes that adorn the Green Lady seem to go on into infinity. Mila finds herself seized suddenly by a ripple of fear— suppose the surface were to turn to solid ice before she could return? Suppose the sun fell from the sky and boiled the sea?

But such panic always seizes her when she's so deep beneath the waves. Man wasn't meant for the sea. Shafir told her that, too.

"No matter how we yearn to return to it, we made the mistake of crawling out of the water a long, long time ago, and the ocean isn't quick to forgive such an insult. We may always feel a part of it, but it will have no part of us."

Mila angles herself downward and kicks. She's been down here maybe five turns of the small water clock; she has perhaps fifteen left, if she uses her energy wisely. There's no rush.

Beneath the white building rest two more layers of foundation, and beneath that, a pale white star that is almost too large for Mila to make out its tapered points, but she knows that they are there. She swims until she can rest her palms along the star's face, feeling its age, its ancientness.

There's something in the dark—isn't there always?— and it only catches her eye because it lies under a fleeting shaft of sunlight from above. Squinting through the fine sheen of sand that her kicking feet disturbed, Mila pulls herself closer to the star. A small piece of metal rests upon the face, attached to a little ring. It has a shape she's never seen before. She reaches for it and grasps it in her hand somewhat tentatively, unsure of what she expects— perhaps it will burn her, perhaps the seafloor will open and swallow her up for attempting to steal a precious treasure— but the trinket settles against her palm and she slips her thumb through the little ring. Nothing else happens.

She meant to swim between the Green Lady's feet, and hug the folds of the great woman's metal robes, but excitement at her little find makes her blood boil and Mila kicks for the surface, forcing herself to hover at intervals and blow a stream of bubbles through her nose. The surface breaks around her head— no ice to be found— and she gasps and coughs when water rushes into her mouth.

"Mila?" The rope ladder drops off the edge of the dock, and she grasps it. "You're back already?"

She climbs quickly, her muscles screaming as she frees herself of the water; it clings to her limbs like it's trying to keep her there a little longer. The dock's wooden planks radiate the sun's heat, and she collapses upon them gratefully.

"I found something."

"What?"

She's not sure. She opens her palm and examines the little piece of metal. Perhaps once it was painted— she thinks she sees a fleck of red here, white there— but she can see the faint lines of an engraving, though the sea has worn it down. Squinting, she holds it up to the light.

I ♡ nyc

"What's it mean? What's it say?" Wren asks, and Mila jumps; she was so engrossed in the trinket that she didn't realize her friend had stretched out beside her.

"I don't know. Shafir?" Mila extends the odd artifact to their companion. "Do you know what this means?"

Shafir takes it and runs her fingers around its edges, along the circumference of the little ring, and finally across the engraving. "Oh," she says, very quietly. "New York."

"What's that?"

"A place. The Green Lady's home."

"This place? Where the Forest is now?"

"Yes."

Wren whistles. "Mila— you found something from the Before."

Fear electrifies Mila's fingertips. She clambers to her feet and takes the artifact back from Shafir, staring down at it in wonder. Whatever New York was, it's down there now, with the feet of the Green Lady.

"It burned," Shafir murmurs. Her arms are still wrapped around her knees. She begins to rock back and forth. "The world burned, and the last uncharted island turned to water, and the sea rose and swallowed up Those Who Came Before, and they fled as far as they could, they left for the stars, but they left Us behind, and our skin turned dark while the sun grew hot—" She keeps talking, but in words that make no sense to Mila's ear. The scholars bear a curse. The price they pay for knowledge is the madness of knowing.

Mila extends her arm back as far as she could, her small, lean body arcing with the effort, and hurls the trinket. It sails through the air, winking in the sunlight, and lands in the water with a decided little plop. From New York had it come, and to New York did it return.

"Come on," Mila says shakily. She dons her tunic and her shoes and pulls Shafir to her feet. She and Wren walk the scholar home.

582

"They're Purging us." Kilik blinked, his nails moving up and down on his thighs, up and down, up and down, rapid, rat-a-tat motion. His eyes flicked this way and that, focusing on Siris's face, then away, at an indistinct point over his friend's shoulder.

Siris swallowed around the thickness in her throat. "Who?"

"*Us*. Me and you. Our people."

"Mine or yours?"

"*All of us*."

Siris drew in a long, slow breath. Her ears twitched. A shiver took root at the base of her skull and travelled the full seven feet of her spine, vibrating down to the tip of her tail. Kilik trembled beside her, nails scraping along the metal edges of his heater, fiddling with the controls, increasing the temperature, superheating his own blood.

"They can't do that," Siris said at length. "Between the Kadari and the Sinx'ja alone—"

"I know. Damn, I know. But it won't stop them. You know it won't."

She couldn't argue that. Her tail flicked. "We're talking… what, two million citizens?"

"Yep. Yep. Two mill. At least." Kilik made a high chittering noise, tongue flicking out, running along his scaly lips. His neck arched. Siris looked at him, let her eyes travel up and down the purple veins that lined the softness of his throat. "Where are we supposed to go? That's the question. Where in all of Creation are we supposed to go?" He keened, turned up his heater some more. "We were here first!"

Yes, they were. When Man made the Kadari and the Sinx'ja and all of His other bastardized excuses for creatures, these chimeric splice-races that hovered somewhere between animal and man, He had put them on this world, on Ios, and vowed to leave them in peace.

And leave them in peace He had, until Earth could no longer sustain over ten billion miserable carbon sacks. The planet swelled and teemed with life until it spilled over the edges, until the resources began to dwindle. Man sucked His world dry, and then the strongest and the smartest and the most fertile came to Ios.

Siris tipped her head back, sniffing at the wind. No scent of Man here. The Walls were equipped with negative pressure vents. The respective atmospheres of the Chimeric Sector and the Human Sector never mixed. From the roof of her apartment complex, she and Kilik could see in all directions, and in all directions stood the Wall, hiding them from the Human world.

"How are they going to do it?"

"Who knows? Who knows?" Kilik wrung his hands. He was a 'lizard.' His genes came from a tiny little 'gecko' from Earth. Siris was told she was a 'lynx.' That was how education began for the Chimera. They were given a picture of a creature from Earth and told "This is you. You're an animal. You've been given Human genes, and you should be thankful."

But Siris didn't think she was an animal. She recognized her reflection in the mirror. She knew her name. She could do complex mathematics. She had elucidated a protein structure for a Human lab when Their biologists couldn't figure it out.

And, when she looked at Kilik, something happened to her heart. It quickened and ached. Did animals feel like that? She didn't think so.

"Think they'll cut off the Factor?"

Siris's blood chilled. "No. They wouldn't."

"What if they did?" Kilik shifted, reaching for his heater again, but he'd already maxed it out. Was he really still cold? "The withdrawal effects alone would be enough to…"

"Don't." Siris grabbed his hand a touch too quickly, and he looked at her, his wide mouth twisting in concern. She looked down at her feet. She had seen what withdrawal did to the Chimera. She had seen Kadari writhing in pain, screaming, clawing at their chests and bellies, spilling their own intestines onto the pristine laboratory floors, when she cleaned up their previously sterile rooms the blood soaked into her fur—

"Hey, I'm sorry." Kilik's hand tightened. He had long, spindly fingers. His hands were somewhat sticky. They adhered to hers. "I'm sorry, I shouldn't have said that."

No, he shouldn't have, but she forgave him. She always forgave Kilik, because his anxiety was out of his control. It controlled him, and she would never fault him for that. She squeezed his hand.

"It's alright."

Siris was less than her Human counterparts. There had never been any question of that in her mind. Not even a ghost of a doubt. They were overlords, creators. She depended on Man for everything; for the clean air behind the Walls, for the Factor-infused drugs that would keep her genes from coming undone, that kept her Human immune system from attacking her Chimeric body. She depended on Man for her work, her research. Without Man, she had neither living nor life.

She looked up from her computer, peering through the two-way mirror at Subject 582. 582 was a 'thylacine,' whatever that was; he didn't look like any Chimera she'd ever seen before. 582 was purely experimental, resurrected from preserved tissues from an animal that had gone extinct on Earth hundreds of years before splicing began.

And 582 was dying.

Siris lowered her gaze, made a note on his blood pressure, which had been steadily climbing for the last three weeks. 582 presented with extreme aggression, cancerous lesions on his throat and groin and under his arms, and excessive bleeding from injuries, of which he had many. In fits of rage, he would throw himself against the walls of his cell, claw at his arms and scratch at the lesions until they opened and bled. He could neither speak nor write; Siris sometimes wondered if he was even capable of thought. 582 had been born and raised in a lab in the Human sector. He had been transferred so Siris could observe his response to a new form of Factor, a different isotope which was apparently cheaper to produce.

It didn't work. Siris had known that since she'd administered the first dose. She had requested a termination of the experiment, suggested that 582 be returned to the Human sector so behavioral studies could continue. The new Factor doesn't work, she emphasized.

But the Human Sector didn't want 582 back. They had what they needed from him. Double-check the Factor, They told her. Run the test out until the end.

The end, in this case, meant 582's death.

Siris swallowed and pulled on one of her ears. She couldn't look away from 582 for more than a few moments at a time. He drew her gaze, and she watched his agony with dark fascination. It would be over soon. She told herself that over and over, again and again, a drumming mantra that beat its fists against the inside of her skull. It would be over soon. 582 would die. His body would tear itself apart.

Contact between researchers and their subjects was strictly prohibited. Siris had enforced this rule with almost ruthless intensity. She never spoke to her subjects—not when they begged her for mercy, not when they asked to be released, not when they asked to see their families, not when they asked for their Factor, right before withdrawal took hold.

But now she pressed a wavering fingertip to the red button on her console, and heard the crackle of static over the speaker in 582's room. He twitched his head, lips drawing up off his teeth, and snarled up at the innocuous box in the corner. She sometimes played music over the speaker, as part of behavioral studies. It was particularly interesting to observe the ebb and flow of 582's aggression when she played music of different genres.

"Subject 582?"

He didn't waver. He continued to stare at the speaker, his hackles raised.

"Is that your name?"

No reply.

"Do you have a different name?"

Nothing.

"Can you speak?"

And more nothing.

"Do you mind if I give you a name? Can I call you Ece?" Ece had been her favorite subject, a little Kandari who was subjected to withdrawals to test yet another "affordable" Factor. He had lived. That was why he was her favorite.

582 howled and leapt at the box, missed it, of course, by several feet, and hit the ground. Grunting, he struggled to his feet, little droplets of bright red blood landing on the floor. He sat back on his haunches and began to claw at his face and ears, screaming.

Siris turned off the speaker.

News of the Purge hit official channels two days later. Kilik had gotten the news from his boss; he served as an aide to the Governor, a towering Simia, one of the few lucky Chimera to be spliced from a 'gorilla.' The Simia were closest to the Humans, not quite Their brethren, but perhaps Their distant cousins. They certainly wouldn't be Purged.

But the Kadari and Sinx'ja, the Governor said, his great hairy brows knitted together, were going to leave.

The official message was thus: Ios was a small world, and another group of colonists was being ferried from Earth. The Humans needed more room, and the Chimera deserved a world where they could flourish and thrive in freedom. This was a kindness, Man insisted. They had raised the Chimera with love and attention, but all 'birds' must someday leave the nest.

Siris laughed when Kilik told her. She laughed until she cried. Because sending two million creatures off-planet would take an entire fleet, ships equipped with Casimir drives so they could jump to the next system, and fuel and water and food and medicine. And the Humans needed those resources.

When a subject died, their remaining allotment of Factor was locked up in storage. Siris had seen one hundred and ninety-three subjects into their mass graves. She had enough Factor to last years. The day after the announcement, she waited until her colleagues went home before opening the storage and taking a month's worth of Factor. She whittled away a month at a time. Her own supply of Factor began to run low. When she received her new allotment, she ran it through a mass spectrometer, analyzed its structure. It was the correct Factor.

So the Purge had yet to begin.

The first ones to be Purged had been the Risen, nearly fifteen years ago. They were androids, self-contained AI that were born in computers as lines of code, then transferred to walking shells. They came in all forms and shapes and colors. They were everywhere. Like the Chimera, they were lesser, but only in name. The Risen were smart. Everyday they grew smarter. They didn't require food or resources, and their batteries were good for several hundred years.

Ada, a behavioral scientist in Siris's lab, and a 'lizard' like Kilik, had managed to quantify the Risen's progress and map it onto a graph. Siris still remembered the dramatic curve of the exponential function, the way it stretched and reached for the y-axis in a sharp upturn.

"*Hyper* hyperbolic," Ada had said, looking at her work with awe. She had shown Siris a second chart, one much less impressive, a slow, crawling curve that seemed in no rush to reach for infinity. "And here's Man. The Risen will outstrip Them within the next decade."

And so the Risen were Purged. They received regular updates from the Interspecies Relations Department, new software that would better equip them to assist their Human creators. One update contained a virus. The Risen installed it and deactivated. Seven point five million units, gone in mere moments.

A unit called Damascus worked in Siris's lab. Siris missed it dearly, but she hadn't been surprised to see it deactivate. Threats to Human progress, Human supremacy, were wiped out without remorse.

Then Enlightened replaced the Risen seven years later. But the Enlightened were SI—synthetic intelligence. They could not change. They could not grow or evolve or adapt, and someday the universe would move on without them.

They were, like Ece, temporal, fleeting things, but Siris didn't pity them. The universe would someday leave her behind, too.

Kilik became increasingly anxious. He overworked his heater until it broke, and shelled out two months' worth of credits to purchase a new one (not that he could live without it; just another way the Humans kept him trapped). Siris took on the burden of helping him come down from those peaks of panic, brought him back to the gentle valleys where they could be together, where they passed idle hours talking about the future, their futures, their future. Their future, until this point, had been some distant mayhaps, an unspoken promise. But that was back when the future was infinite. Now it was a discrete segment of time, something that had a beginning and an inevitable end. It would come and it would go, with or without them, so three days after the official announcement, they took hold and vowed not to let go.

"I still wonder how it'll happen," Kilik mused. He let his feet dangle over the edge of the roof, watching the twin suns dip below the Walls. He drummed his nails upon his heater.

"Don't. It's not worth the worry." Siris trailed her fingertips down his back, but the port embedded at the base of his tail gave her pause. It connected to his heater via a super-insulated tube. The tube was full of his blood. Its twin embedded itself just beneath the slim arches of his collar. "Does it hurt? Having these things in you?"

"No. Or maybe it does, and I've just stopped feeling them." His touch upon the heater was almost tender. An unfortunate side-effect of the splice. All Sinx'ja wore the heaters, because a body that towered eight feet tall with a messy hybrid circulatory system somewhere between a reptile's and a simian's couldn't possibly be expected to heat itself. The metabolics of each discrete organism, Ada had once said, were the biological mechanisms most severely debilitated by splicing.

Siris looked down at her own body, at the curious blend of the feline and the hairless ape. She wondered about what was growing inside her, whether the microbiota that populated her lower intestine were anything like a Human's.

It didn't merit much thought. Either way, she'd be gone soon, she and Kilik both. They had briefly entertained wild imaginings of a rebellion, a revolution that would shake the the world to its knobbly knees. *"I have no interest in maintaining the status quo. I want to overthrow it."* Some Human had said that. She had a name—Machiavelli?—but it held no meaning for her.

At the end of the night, though, all that mattered was togetherness. Them.

A Human came from beyond the Wall. He was a young man, tall and wiry, with straight dark hair and eyes the color of a storm. He came to visit Siris in her lab, explained that he was a diplomat, a politician assigned to Kadari-Human relations. He watched 582 with his mouth hanging open, his eyes widening as 582 thrashed and screamed and threw himself against the walls of his sterile prison.

"My God. This is monstrous."

Siris looked up at him. "What?"

The diplomat looked at her, blinking rapidly. His name was Nicholas. She remembered that about him and little else. "How can you bear to see him like this?"

Lacking an answer, she tugged on her ear and looked back down at her monitor. Nicholas crossed the room in wide strides and leaned over to look at her data, his hands clasped behind his back. She rather liked the way he carried himself, with a straight back and proud shoulders, his eyes focused forward, always forward.

"What are you studying?"

Siris shifted in her seat, tail flicking back and forth across the floor, leaving little trails in the dust. "Um. Behavioral abnormalities."

"As a result of what?"

"Experimental splicing." Siris brightened the lights in 582's room so Nicholas could have a better look. "Do you know what he is?"

"The Tasmanian tiger, of course."

"No—he's a 'thylacine.'"

Nicholas smiled at her, not unkindly. "They're the same thing. They went extinct on Earth well over seven hundred years ago. The footage of the last specimen is famous." He looked back up at 582, his mouth pulling downward in what Siris recognized as an expression of sadness, or distaste. "Why they didn't just clone new specimens from the preserved tissue, why they felt the need to make a new Chimeric breed…"

"What?"

He straightened and ran a hand through his hair. "He looks a lot more like the original animal than you do. I mean, you have, you know—" He swept a hand over his face and shrugged. "Humanoid features. Animal body, human features. He really looks more beast than man."

"Oh."

Nicholas made a face, the corners of his mouth drawing back until his mouth formed a hard line. "Sorry. I know I sound like an ignorant ass. This is my first time talking to a Chimeric… girl? You're a girl, right? You're pretty enough to be a— do the Chimera have gender? And *cis-* and *trans-* identities? Or…?"

Siris giggled. "Yes. We have gender. I'm female. *Cis*."

"Oh. Good." And he made a strange gesture, his lips lifting to expose his close-set teeth. "I could only handle so much humiliation in one conversation."

Nicholas became a near-constant presence in the lab. He usually filled their hours with chatter; on the rare occasions when he managed to be silent, he liked to watch her work. They talked. They talked about the world beyond the Wall, about the nature of Humanity and the nature of the Chimera. One day, in what was perhaps an error in judgement, she asked a question.

"What do you think about my people, Nicholas? About the Chimera."

He looked up from her notes on a previous subject and his mouth turned into that line again. "What do you mean?"

"Your first visit here, you wondered why the Human Sector created a Chimera from thylacine DNA, instead of a pure specimen. Why?"

Nicholas closed her notes and steepled his fingers, resting his mouth against them. "I don't begrudge your existence, Siris. Not in the slightest. I think your people are fascinating."

Siris blinked, unsure of how to respond. "Um. Thank you."

"No, I don't need thanks. Keep them. My fascination is just evidence of separation, and that's—well—" He waved his hand at her, a gesture she couldn't place. "I like the Chimera. I do. I enjoy their company. I enjoy their cultures and their perspectives." She didn't yet trust her interpretation of Human expressions, but she thought his face softened a little. "I have immensely enjoyed getting to know *you*. But I question the ethics of Chimeric existence. I wonder whether man should have created them to begin with. Whether we… *overstepped*."

"But… Humanity has benefited from our existence, has it not? We do the things Humans don't want to do."

Nicholas canted his head to the side. She could no longer read his body language, his expressions. His movements told her nothing. "And you don't—you don't have a problem with that?"

Siris stared at him, dumbstruck. "Of course I…" But did she? Hadn't she been sitting in this lab, unquestioning, performing every task the Humans sent her way, collecting tedious amounts of data, torturing 582—Ece—because that was what she was told to do? And something cold and hard settled in her stomach, the glacial horror that accompanies the realization of one's place in a system where equality is but a word.

Nicholas watched her, his grey eyes a mystery, and then he leaned forward and touched his mouth to hers. She didn't understand the gesture—there were a thousand things about Humans that she didn't understand— so she sat still and waited for him to finish. When he drew away, his face had hardened with that *something* she recognized as determination.

"Alright," he said, and he bobbed his head up and down. "Alright. I know what to do. Thank you, Siris. And I'm sorry." He headed for the door, swinging his heavy coat around his shoulders, and his footsteps echoed down the hall, carrying him away.

At a loss, Siris turned to the two-way mirror and reached out, placed her palm upon the cool surface. "I don't know, Ece," she said quietly. "I just don't know anymore."

Ece gnawed on his fingers.

The timeframe for the Exodus officially spanned the next three weeks, but the interstellar transport services didn't mobilize, and no one came to help the Chimera close down their cities and pack away their research and industry. It was clear—to Siris, at least—that the Humans had no intention of safely evacuating the Chimera. They were going to be wiped out. Purged. And though she knew she wasn't the only one who knew the truth, her world kept moving as always, unchanging, quiet and calm. Was it some supreme denial, or were her people really so ignorant? Did anyone really believe that the humans were offering them salvation, another world all their own? Fear, she supposed, was the ultimate paralytic.

She sat in her office, musing, running models for the structure of a novel protein she'd found in Ece's blood. Proteomics were no longer her specialty—the Humans needed behavioral scientists, and she'd complied—but working on structures still comforted her, set her mind at ease. She liked the puzzles.

"Siris." Kilik stuck his head in through the door. "You'll want to see this."

"What is it?"

"That Human—Nicholas—he's on the television."

She got to her feet, curious, and followed him into their sitting room. Nicholas's narrow face peered out at her from their fuzzy screen—the Walls badly interfered with the signal—and his eyes made her breath catch, just a little. Kilik seemed not to notice. He sat down on their couch, drumming his nails on his heater, and she sat at his side.

Nicholas sat across from an older man, his hands folded neatly in his lap, his lips pressed in their hard line. The old man was talking, waving his hands around as he spoke, his voice rising and falling like ocean waves, and Nicholas watched him with what Siris realized was a cold, calculated expression.

"You can spew rhetoric all you want," Nicholas said, and the way the old man drew back told Siris that he'd been interrupted, even if she was still learning how to interpret human speech patterns. It was a little difficult to understand what they were saying; Nicholas had taken great care to use Kadari dialect when he visited her lab. Subtitles ran along the bottom of the screen. Reluctant though she was to look away from his face, she dropped her gaze to the text. "But the Chimera aren't just science experiments. They aren't relics of a far-gone age. They are *evolving*, Jim, just like you and I. They have culture, societal structures, families, relationships, athletic competition, games, music, art, science."

"Surely these are all just derivatives of what we taught them?"

Nicholas shook his head back and forth—negative. A rejection of this man Jim's words. Siris felt a little proud of herself for figuring it out. "I looked at a piece of sheet music. Those temporal patterns aren't present in our musical structures. They use notes that, to our ears, are subaural. Their poetry doesn't follow any meter or pattern I've ever encountered in human literature, and I've been a student of poetry my entire life, Jim, ever since I learned to read when I was four. I met a Kadari scientist—"

"I'm sorry—Kadari?"

"They look like cats. This particular young lady was spliced from a lynx."

"Surely, Nic, 'young lady'—"

"It's Nicholas, and yes, that's appropriate. She identifies as a *cis*-female, Jim, and I'm going to refer to her as such. This young lady has elucidated over fourteen novel protein structures that completely stumped our proteomic specialists. She was never taught how to solve these structures, she simply learned on her own. The mathematics and sub-cellular physics involved are *intuitive* to her."

Jim shuffled several papers on his lap and fidgeted in his seat. "How many different, er, races did you encounter?"

"I met a great many Chimera beyond the Wall. Kadari, of course, in addition to Sinx'ja—a reptilian people—and many Simia, with whom we should all be familiar, as we have a healthy diplomatic relationship with their people. I also met delegates from a race called Quet-zal, who were spliced from birds. Their emperor was, I believe, spliced from fossil-recovered archaeopteryx DNA—"

"I'm sorry, Nic, to keep interrupting you, but—*emperor*?"

"Yes, and it's Nicholas," Nicholas said, and even Kilik couldn't miss the impatience in his voice. "Emperor. Different races utilize different governing structures. Sinx'ja government, for example, closely resembles that of the First Nations people in the American continents on Earth, while Simia use a republican system. But remember, Jim, that they have all been denied access to information on human history and culture—they derived these government structures *all on their own*. And they work. There is no warfare between the Chimeric races—more than can be said for humanity."

"And to what do you attribute this pacifism? To their simplicity of mind, surely?"

Nicholas's nostrils flared. "No. It is because every Chimeric race has been mercilessly oppressed and subjugated by humanity, and this universal suffering unites them."

Jim stared at him, his feeble old mouth hanging open. Kilik and Siris exchanged glances. Nicholas kept right on talking.

"Our creation of the Chimeric races has long been the subject of ethical debate, but it is our treatment of them *now* that concerns me. We cannot take back the fact that we made them, for better or for worse, but now we have a responsibility to treat them as sovereign races. Our prejudices are poison. We have brought life into this world, miraculous, wondrous life, and they are capable of *extraordinary* things, but only if they are removed from our influence and allowed to flourish independent of human tyranny."

Jim's face had pulled into something between a smile and a grimace—Siris couldn't decide which. "But you realize that's what the Exodus is—"

"There is no Exodus. It's a Purge. We're not sending the Chimeric people off to another world, we're going to wipe them out. You see that, don't you, Jim? We all see that. We're all just too stupid and too scared to admit—"

And then the signal cut out. The screen went black. For several long moments, Siris and Kilik sat in silence.

"They shut it down," Kilik said at last, his voice quiet, shell-shocked. "They shut him down."

"Because he was telling the truth."

"Yes. Because he was telling the truth."

"Kilik?"

"Yes?"

Siris leaned into him and touched their mouths together. He didn't move, and blinked at her when she drew back.

"What was that?"

She pulled on one ear. "I don't know. Nicholas did it."

"Hm." Kilik rubbed his mouth, considering. "I wonder what it means?"

"Maybe he was trying to tell me that he was going to fight—that he was going to say those things. Maybe it was a promise."

"A promise." Kilik tapped his heater. "Yes. That seems right to me."

News of Nicholas's arrest hit the Simian government first, and then it spread like wildfire. Protests exploded to life in the Human sectors; Quet-zal reporters flew over the Walls for the first time in decades and filmed the riots. The Wall guardsmen shot several out of the sky, but they kept flocking, kept turning cameras on the madness beyond the Walls in twisted, horrified fascination.

And then humans started coming. The government offices were swamped with requests for permits. No less than seven human scientists visited Siris in her lab over the course of the next three days, talking to her excitedly about her work (not in behavior, but in *proteomics*), and gaping at Ece while he howled and threw himself against the walls and snarled at the blinking light of the camera.

She didn't see much of Kilik for those three days. The Governor had him working nonstop, filing permit after permit. When he did come home, he ran his spindly fingers under hot water for what seemed like hours, muttering to himself. He was irritable and unapproachable, and Siris felt alone.

She dwelled on Nicholas for long spans of time, wondering where he was, whether he was safe, whether his Human captors had hurt him, whether he had a way to communicate outside of the walls of his prison, assuming he still lived. She had asked one of the visiting scientists about the strange ritual involving their mouths, and he laughed and told her it was just a kiss.

Whatever that meant.

One of them also gave her an audio file containing a musical arrangement by a composer called Vivaldi, a piece titled *Four Seasons*. For the most part, Siris liked it, but in places it seemed to go fuzzy and quiet. Parts of the musical range were, for her, subaural, the way much of the music she liked had gone right over Nicholas's head. She had played a piece for him on her computer, a song about a famous Kadari poet, and he had sat with her headphones on, blinking at the wall, non-expressive (or maybe his face had been a twisted mask of emotion, and she just had to be human to see it).

When it was over, he took her headphones off, gave her a peculiar look, and said "Huh." And that was that.

She listened to *Four Seasons* twelve times and wished she could hear what he heard.

The Exodus/Purge was two weeks away when the Chimeric riots began. Nicholas's words had been an awakening. Hearing the alarm raised on the other side of the Wall forced everyone to shake themselves from their denial. Even humans cared about this, and humans were more content than anyone to do whatever their governments told them to do, believe what they were told to believe. So if that young man was angry, and if the rioters pounding on the Walls were angry, then there must be good reason to take up arms.

The lights went out in the city when the sun dipped below the horizon, and most of the generators were shut down to conserve precious resources, but now fires blazed in the night, from torches and bonfires and looters. Siris lay awake in the dark, nine days after Nicholas's arrest, watching the blooms of yellow and orange outside her window while Kilik slept beside her. The days ran him ragged, and he slept the moment he got home from work. She spent too much of her day in quiet contemplation, and at night her brain was a live wire, tripped and sparking, seeking conduits.

Their communicator began to blink. She leaned over and touched the screen, and it lit up with text. A message from the Governor's office. She reached over to rouse Kilik, but froze when she realized what it said.

We seek Siris

She blinked, rubbed her eyes, pulled on her ears to make sure she wasn't dreaming. Hesitant, she reached for the communicator and keyed in a response.

This is she.

Two minutes' pause, and then a reply.

Be at your door in one hour.

Now she did wake Kilik, her heart in her throat, and he maxed out his heater in record time.

An hour later she stood by her door, Kilik prowling back and forth across the kitchen, his tail sweeping anxious little trails through the crumbs on the floor. Siris was struck by the bizarre and overwhelming urge to knead her paws on his shirt, and resisted. Genetic throwbacks were such a hassle.

Three sharp knocks sounded, and she nearly fainted before grasping at the handle and pulling the door open. Standing in the hall were two towering Simia and, between them, battered and bruised and disheveled, was Nicholas.

The Simia hurried him inside, closing and bolting her door, and ushered them into the sitting room, ordering her to take a seat in her own house. They pushed Nicholas into an armchair and swept the apartment, bolting windows and turning on the opaque filters, pulling the blinds over the blackened glass.

Nicholas watched them with apparent interest, waiting until they disappeared into the bedroom before turning to Siris, the corners of his mouth perking upward. "Hi."

"Hello." She didn't know what else to say; she couldn't take her gaze from his narrow face. His left cheek was purple and black, his lower lip was split, and a gash above his right eyebrow had been roughly and poorly stitched. His hair was longer, and dark stubble lined his jaw and chin. "You look…"

"Terrible. I know. I've been saying the human prison system is in need of reform for fifteen years, and now I have personal and empirical evidence." His lips widened, revealing his teeth, miraculously unbroken. "Did you see my interview?"

"I did." She fidgeted. Discomfort radiated from Kilik in waves; his nails rapped a steady drumbeat on his heater. Rat-a-tat-tat, tat-tat. "Thank you. For the things you said. It was very brave."

"It was necessary." He leaned forward and extended a hand toward Kilik. "You're her partner, yes? Nicholas Mikhailovich."

Kilik stared at his hand, and after a few moments Nicholas withdrew it, glancing at Siris. She offered him what she hoped passed for a smile, which she'd been practicing for just such an occasion. Much to her relief, he returned it, and sat back as the Simia reentered the room.

The twosome took a seat, and explained in their rough, grunting tones that Nicholas had been granted political asylum in the Chimeric territories, and had been broken out of a high-security prison when it was overtaken by armed rioters. Siris listened to the story with wide eyes, her heart thudding higher and higher, climbing her ribs, lodging somewhere at the base of her throat. Kilik's fingers somehow tapped faster.

"So what now?" The question exploded from her, unbidden, her voice too loud in her quiet apartment. Nicholas looked at her sideways. "What about the Purge?"

"Exodus," one of the Simia corrected her, but his response was automatic, preprogrammed, and his expression darkened even as he said it. "The Exodus will proceed as planned. Xhe Mikhailovich will accompany you off Ios."

"By which you mean that I'm going to die however they do," he said, his tone light and pleasant. The Simia both glared at him. "We don't need to pretend otherwise, gentlemen. I know your jobs depend on you upholding our government's story, but what need will you have for employment when our boys come in and clean our bodies off the streets?"

The larger of the Simia stood and brushed off his suit. "You have been granted asylum, Xhe Mikhailovich. Please bear in mind that it can be revoked."

Nicholas smiled and nodded. The Simia tossed around a few dire warnings: keep his presence a secret, do not speak of him to anyone under pain of execution for treason, et cetera, and they left without a word about the Purge. Kilik got up and went to the bathroom to vomit.

"Siris?"

She looked at Nicholas, and the sight of his bruised and broken face made her guts churn. "Yes?"

"Can I ask a favor?"

"Of course."

He grinned and patted his stomach. "I'm absolutely starved."

A week until the Purge, and still no announcement about transportation or provisions. The Human government was no longer even trying, though their fallacious official story held in the media, for the most part. One newscaster stood in the middle of a report on an impending economic crisis and screamed about the Purge. He was shot on camera.

"Damn," Nicholas said as they watched the screen go dark. A moment later, a cheery message about technical difficulties popped up. "It was a good try, Comrade."

The riots continued on both sides of the Wall. Kilik stopped coming home, perpetually tied up in the Governor's office. They had long since stopped issuing permits, but humans still streamed in, fascinated and furious. A few stories broke about humans and Chimera interloping, bribing public officials to sign off on illegal weddings and distribute illegal licenses in the hopes that doing so might save them.

"Like a green-card marriage," Nicholas said with a laugh, "but if you get found out, you die."

His lack of urgency puzzled Siris. His own life was on the line, and had been since he spoke out at the interview, but he mostly idled around her apartment, cooking dinner before she came home from work. He spent his time in front of her television, flipping through channels, watching report after report about the riots, the protests, the screaming of the citizens, and the deafening silence from governments on either end.

"They're going to live, you know," he said suddenly, six days before the Purge, while she poured him a glass of water. He looked better; he'd gained back some weight, the gash on his forehead was mostly healed, and the bruises had faded to a sickly yellow. A few kindly humans had moved in down the hall with their Sinx'ja neighbors and given him a razor and scissors, and he was now neatly groomed. "The Chimeric government officials who cooperate. They'll be allowed to stay."

Siris's throat ran dry. "You mean like Kilik?"

"Maybe. He's just an aide. It's probably up to the Governor."

Which explained Kilik's sudden desire to impress and amaze his boss. Siris drank quietly, feeling Nicholas's eyes on her.

"You love him?"

"What?"

"Kilik." Nicholas set his glass down. "Do you love him?"

She didn't know how to respond, so she didn't, and at length he continued.

"I like you. Maybe more than I should. I think we should escape together."

"Escape where? You'll be shot on sight at the Wall, and I could never get a permit. Even if I could, I couldn't smuggle you past."

He lowered his gaze, rubbing a thumb against the rim of his glass. "Will you keep this a secret?"

"You know I will."

"I talked a little with the people who attacked the prison, before they brought me to the Wall and the Simia smuggled me out. Two days before the Purge, one of the rebel factions is going to blow up a section of the Wall."

She blinked at him. "Really?"

"Really. I know where. If we can get there, I can get us transport off-world."

"But where would we go?"   "Earth," he said, and looked up at her. She was better at reading his face now; his eyes seemed to be on fire. "It's been three hundred years since it was densely populated. The environment has begun to recover. We could farm, grow enough to support ourselves."

She swallowed. "I… I couldn't leave Kilik."

His smile was bitter. "Well, I suppose he'll have to come, too."

They said goodnight after that, and she watched him settle down on the couch before turning out the light. She lay awake for hours afterward, staring at the ceiling, watching the flicker of fires outside. Utter madness out there. She hadn't been to the lab in two days. She hoped the SI was still feeding Ece. She'd have to find a way to put him down. Anything she could come up with was bound to better than however the Humans intended to Purge all of Chimeric kind.

She slept, and wasn't surprised that she had nightmares.

Siris went to the lab the next morning and found Ada dead at her desk, a bullet hole in her head oozing blood. Their hard drives were wiped, their physical data burned or stolen. The SI was nowhere to be found. Several interfaces had been smashed. Only Ece remained, yowling at the camera, chewing on his fingers. Siris carried her friend's body to the dissection room and covered it with a sheet, and then she wept, long and hard, crying out weeks of slowly mounting terror and indecision.

She didn't know why Ada had to die, and with the computers wiped clean, there would never be any way of knowing. She felt a horrible, guilty sense of relief that her friend had never confided in her; if she had, Siris would be dead, too.

She fed and watered Ece, but didn't collect her usual data. No point, now. Even his blood pressure records had been taken. Creation only knew what value they had to whomever had done this. Siris left Ece in his room for the time being and headed for home, numb from the tips of her ears to the pads of her feet.

Nicholas answered the door when she gave the password, and took her into his arms at once, whispering assurances into her ear, guiding her into the apartment and bolting the door. She must look truly awful, she thought, for him to know something was wrong so quickly, or maybe he was just better at reading her than she was at reading him.

He held her for a long time, running slow, smooth caresses down her back, his hand warm against her fur. He didn't ask what had happened, and for that she was grateful; it was too horrible to put into words, at least out loud.

"I'm going," she said at length, looking up at him. "With you. To Earth. Or wherever."

He nodded and kissed her. After a while she took him to bed, a little scared, a little unsure, not convinced that it would even work between them. But it was different than it was with Kilik.

It was better.

"We're leaving. Tomorrow." Siris didn't look up from her lap as she spoke. She could feel the tension in Kilik's frame, heard the soft whine of his heater, turned up too high. "Someone's going to blow a hole in the Wall, and Nicholas and I are going to leave."

"Leave? Where do you think you're going to go?"

"Earth."

Kilik released a short laugh and got to his feet, pacing their bedroom, running a hand over the frills that topped his head. "Earth. That's insane. You know that's insane, right? And you'll never get past the Wall, even if it's got a great gaping hole in it."

Siris closed her eyes and listened to the thudding of her heart. After this conversation, one way or the other, it would all be over—she and Kilik, or she and Nicholas, or both, and the world, and her research, and everything she had ever known—if she could just get through these words.

"Siris." Kilik knelt and took her hands. "Listen. The Governor is impressed with my work. He says he can protect us. You may not know this, but… officials who have been doing their jobs are going to be exempted from the Exodus."

"You mean the Purge."

"The Exodus, Siris, you *must* call it the Exodus."

"Changing the name doesn't change what it is."

He inhaled, his nostrils flaring. "The Governor will make sure that you and I are safe. You don't have to go anywhere, and definitely not with that madman."

"He's not mad."

"His head is full of ideology, Siris. Meaningless rhetoric. It might feel good, but it won't keep you alive."

"It doesn't feel good. It scares me. But I can't stay here," she said, her voice rising. "I won't stay on a world that wanted me dead, Kilik. I can't. I'd rather die than keep living like this, like something *lesser*."

"We *are* lesser, all right? That's just how it is, there's prejudice, that's the status quo, that—" He vented a frustrated sigh, tried to turn up his heater, and found that it was already on its highest setting. "We can accept that and live or fight it and die. I know which I want, Siris. I want to live, with you, forever if I can. Please stay here with me."

She shook her head, trembling.

"What are you doing?"

Oh, Creation. She was doing what Nicholas did, a shake of the head, a rejection, a denial. A motion that said *No*, that said *I won't accept this*. But it was a human thing, not theirs, and Kilik didn't know what it meant.

"I'm going, Kilik. I'm sorry."

"What?" His voice hardened. "Did you—did you sleep with him?"

A nod, and then she remembered. "Yes."

Kilik sat in silence for a moment. He dropped her hands and got to his feet, his nails drumming, ceaseless drumming, rat-a-tat-tat, and then he left the room with wide strides. The front door opened and closed with a slam.

She never saw him again.

"Can we rethink this?"

"No."

Nicholas released a long, slow sigh, sinking down in his seat. "If you insist."

"I do." Siris tugged on her ears, casting another anxious glance into the backseat of their car. Her refrigerated cases of Factor were secured and double-secured.

"Siris… what's going to happen when you run out of that stuff?"

"I can synthesize more if I can get to a working lab. Earth has labs, right?"

Nicholas laughed. She liked the way he laughed, expelling air in hard puffs. Ha, ha, ha. So different from her lilting purr, or Kilik's high chittering noises. Her heart said *rat-a-tat-tat* and ached. "Yes, it does. It might be a while before we can get a power source, though. The equipment won't run until we do."

"I have enough Factor to last a while."

"Good." He squeezed her hand. "And when 582 runs out?"

"Ece. I've been calling him Ece." She tugged on her left ear, which felt a little sore. "He's dying and has been for some time. His Factor is almost out. But I won't leave him here, Nicholas. I can't."

"I understand. I just want to know what we're in for. Is he safe?"

"I honestly don't know."

He grinned, flashed his white teeth. "How exciting."

At her insistence, he waited in the car while she headed into the lab. Her heart thundered behind her ribs, drumming a painful tattoo against the bones. When she swiped her access card through the reader by the door, her hair—all of it—stood on end. Something was amiss. She sensed it in the primal way an animal senses the proximity of predators. And she was animal, after all. But then, so was man.

She entered the lab cautiously, quietly. It remained in its prior state of disarray, but there was an orderliness to some parts of the chaos that made her pulse quicken. The debris wasn't littered quite so randomly; chairs and fallen cabinets had been pushed back toward the wall. Ada's body was gone. Someone—or a great many someones—had entered since she was here last.

Something creaked in the lab, and she froze. Said someone was still in residence, it seemed.

"C'mere. Son of a bitch— c'*mere*!"

A howl, unmistakably Ece's. Siris froze and dropped to a crouch, her heart wriggling in her throat, and for one wild moment she considered turning heel and running, just running, escaping to the car and letting Nicholas take her as far as they could go.

But she was all Ece had.

Siris crept into the lab, edging around the door—already ajar—and peering through the two way mirror. A man stood in Ece's room, holding a gun in one hand and trying to slip a collar on the end of a long stick around Ece's neck. The subject—man? Victim? Beast?—cowered in the corner, lips pulled back from his teeth in a snarl, eyes narrowed and trained upon the gun.

"C'mere," the man grunted again, and advanced on his captive. Ece bristled, hunkering against the wall, bringing one mutilated hand to his snarling teeth and gnawing upon his fingers.

Siris cast a look around the room. Something, anything, before this animal put a bullet between Ece's eyes— there. Fire extinguisher. She lowered herself to her belly and crawled across the floor, beneath the man's line of sight, and jimmied the extinguisher out from beneath a toppled chair. She squinted in the gloom at the directions on the side, but they were in some tongue of man that she had never learned to read. She fingered the pin in the side, tugged experimentally on the trigger. Such a simple mechanism, surely…

Cradling the exstinguisher to her chest, Siris squirmed toward the broken door to Ece's room. She was just angling the nozzle into the room when Ece howled and, almost in the same breath, the gun went off with a crack that made Siris' ears ring. Face screwed up in pain, she clapped both hands to her ears, pressing her mouth to the cold linoleum floor to muffle a cry.

The pain threatened to shatter her skull, but, eyes streaming, Siris pushed herself to her feet and pulled the pin out of the extinguisher. She pulled two deep breaths before leaping into Ece's room. Without letting her attention linger too long on the fresh blood on the floor, or the sheer *size* of the intruder's gun, she shouted at him— "*Hey*!" but she only felt her lips form the word, she couldn't hear it— and he turned on her, mouth opening in a surprised 'o' beneath a thick moustache, eyebrows raising above the rim of dark sunglasses, and Siris pulled the trigger.

Nothing happened.

She thought—in a very dim, far-away sort of way—that she shouldn't be surprised. When had the lab last had a safety inspection? Did anyone care if the Chimera had a working fire extinguisher? Did anyone care if they went up in flames? Of course not. Of *course* not. Man had fire extinguishers. Man could light fires for fun and have enough extinguishers to stop the conflagration. Chimera had more fires and fewer extinguishers but man would never extend a hand to help, because it was *easier* for man to assume that the Chimera could take care of themselves, that those occasional fires were their fault anyway, than it was to admit that man had systemically oppressed another race for so, so long, that those infernos would burn on and on because man was careless and callous—that they would burn until someone like Nicholas, someone who *looked like them*, stood up and screamed at the injustice—

She should have died there, holding her useless fire extinguisher and hating and loving but *hating*, and the intruder lifted his gun and his stupid 'o' mouth became a hard, angry line and she couldn't see his eyes behind his sunglasses but she knew the look he wore, knew the disdain and the utter, chilling lack of empathy— she should have died, but Ece, covered in blood, sprang forward and hit the intruder and they both tumbled to the ground in a mess of flailing limbs.

"*Ece!*" She moved forward, trying to see where man ended and Chimera began, but that gun swung up in an arc and the finger squeezed the trigger in the same moment she went to the floor. The bullet went high, taking out a piece of the door frame, but this time her ears were the only casualty. She called for Ece again around the *eeeeee* buzzing in her skull.

And Ece looked at her. Directly. His eyes locked on hers. Her heart stopped. And his snarling mouth moved in a way she'd *never* seen before, those yellow eyes flashed and he *shouted at her.*

"*Go!*"

Siris stared.

Subject 582 threw his head back and howled. To her dying day—and Siris would live another eighty-six point four years, exactly, on a farm that she and Nicholas would start together, tending a little patch of greenery that would grow, and grow, big enough to sustain the fourteen Chimera who found their way to Earth ten years after they did, who picked up the broken pieces of their lives and started anew, formed families and had children, children who married and had children of their own, and their community grew up and flourished around a little patch of green— to her dying day Siris remembered that howl, the howl that tore at her heart and viscera and made her skin crawl and her bones burn.

"My name is Ece!"

He threw himself upon the intruder, fangs sinking down on the man's exposed throat, and Siris turned and ran before the arteries burst and before the blood sprayed high and wide, covering Ece's muzzle and painting his teeth.

"Siris!" Nicholas stood at the top of the stairs, eyes wide, his hair battered by the wind, his skin pale. "I heard gunshots—is everything—"

Siris flung herself into his arms and pushed him back, away from the lab, from the stairs, toward their car.

"Siris, what—"

"Go."

"What?"

"Ece said to go."

Nicholas let himself be led, his hand tight and sweaty in hers. "*Ece* said?"

She threw his door open and crawled across his seat to get behind the wheel. He clambered in after her, pulling his door shut, and she depressed the gas pedal to the floor, ignoring his shout of panic when their car peeled out and she pulled it away from the lab at nearly a ninety-degree angle.

"Where are we going?"

"What? Siris, what are you—where's—isn't Ece coming?"

"No." She set her jaw, tightening both hands around the wheel. "So where is it? This hole they're going to blow in the Wall."